JOE COLTON'S JOURNAL

My marriage is self-destructing before my eyes. How can the woman I've loved for a lifetime have changed so much? I hardly recognize her anymore. Good thing I have Tripp Calhoun's visit to lift my spirits. Who would have guessed that the troubled teenage gang banger who first showed up at the Hopechest Ranch would grow up to be a caring doctor? He's done us all proud. He's in Prosperino for business—and to attend the wedding of a former flame. Pride demands that he make an appearance, and he's sweet-talked my daughter, Amber, into being his trophy date. Those two are so good at "pretending" that the sizzling electricity they generate is powerful enough to heat up the entire Hacienda de Alegria Estate! Too bad the hardheaded Tripp isn't looking to settle down with a "pampered" Colton heiress. But come on, now. His true feelings are more transparent than Meredith's totally inappropriate new wardrobe. And if I can see the writing on the wall, it's just a matter of time before my savvy daughter does, too....

About the Author

SANDRA STEFFEN

Two things Sandra Steffen loves are challenges and happy endings. What could be more challenging than throwing a spoiled heiress and a struggling young doctor with a chip on his shoulder together in a pretend engagement? That's exactly what happens in *The Trophy Wife*. Sparks fly, tempers flare and of course love finds a way...or does it? This national bestselling author and winner of the 1994 National Readers' Choice Award was up for the challenge and is immensely proud of Tripp and Amber's story.

Sandra grew up in Michigan in a large, close-knit family. In keeping with this tradition, she and her husband are the proud parents of four sons.

The Trophy Wife

Sandra Steffen

Published by Silhouette Books

America's Publisher of Contemporary Romance

Special thanks and acknowledgment are given
to Sandra Steffen for her contribution
to THE COLTONS series.

SILHOUETTE BOOKS
300 East 42nd St.,
New York, N. Y. 10017

ISBN 0-373-38713-X

THE TROPHY WIFE

This edition published by arrangement with Harlequin Books S.A.

® and TM are trademarks of Harlequin Books S.A., used under license. Trademarks indicated with ® are registered in the United States Patent and Trademark Office, the Canadian Trade Marks Office and in other countries.

Visit Silhouette at www.eHarlequin.com

Printed in U.S.A.

THE
COLTONS

Meet the Coltons—
a California dynasty with a legacy of privilege and power.

Tripp Calhoun: *The deceptive doctor.* Anxious to save face in front of an old girlfriend, this pediatrician needs a date for one night...and gorgeous, accomplished Amber Colton seems the answer to his prayers.

Amber Colton: *The trophy date.* This sophisticated businesswoman's eyes had been wide open when she agreed to be the doctor's date for one night. But now that their contract has ended, she'd like to make their agreement a lot more binding....

Meredith Colton: *The missing mother.* Desperate to believe the fantastic story she's just been told, this amnesia victim has a sudden flashback and knows her true identity. Now she's just waiting for the right moment to return to Prosperino.

THE COLTONS

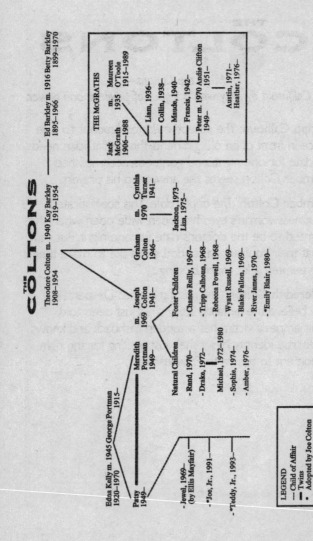

THE McGRATHS

Jack McGrath 1906–1988 m. 1935 Maureen O'Toole 1915–1989
- Liam, 1936–
- Collin, 1938–
- Maude, 1940–
- Francis, 1942–
- Peter m. 1970 Andie Clifton 1949–   1951–
  - Austin, 1971–
  - Heather, 1976–

Ed Barkley 1895–1966 m. 1916 Betty Barkley 1899–1970

Theodore Colton 1908–1954 m. 1940 Kay Barkley 1919–1954

Joseph Colton 1941– m. 1969

Cynthia Turner 1941– m. 1970
- Jackson, 1973–
- Liza, 1975–

Graham Colton 1946–

Edna Kelly 1920–1970 m. 1945 George Portman 1915–

Meredith Portman 1949–

Patsy 1949–

Foster Children
- Chance Reilly, 1967–
- Tripp Calhoun, 1968–
- Rebecca Powell, 1968–
- Wyatt Russell, 1969–
- Blake Fallon, 1969–
- River James, 1970–
- *Emily Blair, 1980–

Natural Children
- Rand, 1970–
- Drake, 1972–
- Michael, 1972–1980
- Sophie, 1974–
- Amber, 1976–

- Jewel, 1969– (by Ellis Mayfair)
- *Joe, Jr., 1991–
- *Teddy, Jr., 1993–

LEGEND
- Child of Affair
• Twins
* Adopted by Joe Colton

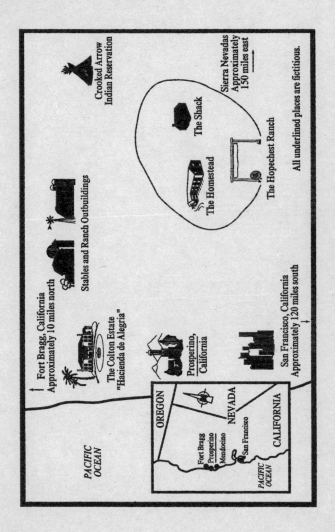

Crooked Arrow
Indian Reservation

Sierra Nevadas
Approximately
150 miles east

The Shack

Stables and Ranch Outbuildings

The Homestead

The Hopechest Ranch

All underlined places are fictitious.

Fort Bragg, California
Approximately 10 miles north

The Colton Estate
"Hacienda de Alegria"

Prosperino,
California

PACIFIC
OCEAN

OREGON

NEVADA

CALIFORNIA

Fort Bragg
Prosperino
Mendocino
San Francisco

PACIFIC
OCEAN

CALIFORNIA

San Francisco, California
Approximately 120 miles south

One

Amber Colton stared at her bare feet. Her nail polish was chipped on the big toenail of her left foot. She sighed. She checked her fingernails and sighed again. There had to be more to life than nail polish.

If she listened hard enough, she could hear the ocean. She could smell it on the air, too, but she couldn't feel it. Whether it had been due to luck or planning, this portion of the garden was protected from the cool wind that could blow in off the ocean at a moment's notice no matter what the season.

Looping one arm around her bent knees, she shaded her eyes and studied the cotton-candy clouds in the sky. There was a time when finding clouds shaped like elephants, mushrooms and all sorts of other objects had kept her and her brothers and sisters busy for hours at a time. Back then, the patio surrounding the pool had been wet constantly from so many children splashing, and voices, sometimes a dozen at a time, rang through the courtyard.

And Amber had never been bored.

She pushed a shock of her strawberry-blond hair away from her face and rose to her feet. She never should have come home in this mood. She should have taken her friends up on their invitation to go to the Cayman Islands with them. But she just couldn't muster up enough enthusiasm to brave the airsickness that inevitably plagued her when she flew, just to watch the sun go down from another hemisphere.

It was the same sun. The same life. The same feeling of restlessness that threatened to drive her to tears. No, not to tears. Amber Colton didn't cry, not anymore.

At twenty-six she was far too young for boredom and restlessness to become a permanent condition. It would pass. She shouldn't have taken today off, that's all. But lately despite the fact that her work at the Hopechest Foundation was meaningful and worthwhile, she felt as if something was missing, and had been for a long time. She'd had vacation time to use up and she'd been missing her dad something awful, so she'd driven out from Fort Bragg to her childhood home in Prosperino to visit him. Still, Amber felt terribly alone. And bored. God, yes, she was bored.

She'd been bored last night, too. Her friend Claire Davis must have heard it in her voice when Amber had called her last night. Claire had shown up at the ranch at five this morning. Amber glanced at the woman who was sleeping soundly in the shade on the other side of the pool. Claire was a good friend. Amber sighed. A good friend who just happened to be nocturnal.

She didn't know what prompted her to peer into the backyard. A tiny bit of color caught her eye. For lack of any clear plan, she meandered to the edge of the formal-looking path.

Other than the ornamental and showy variety, there weren't many flowers in the garden anymore. Once upon a time, her mother had spent hours on end filling the garden with lush green foliage and flowering plants native to California. For the past ten years, the gardening had been another of poor Marco's responsibilities. He managed to keep it fairly neat and tidy, but the riot of beautiful yet casual colorful flowers was but a memory these days.

Amber bent down. The tiny pink blossoms nearly hidden from view were more than a mere memory. Somehow, the plants had survived all these years of neglect. Curiosity sent Amber to her knees. From there, it was easy to get down on all fours and stretch out until she could reach the weeds growing behind the ornamental shrubs that had taken the place of her mother's flowers.

From this angle, Amber discovered more delicate blooms hidden among the weeds. Intrigued by the tenacity of the little plants, she ignored the hot sun at her back and the hard ground beneath her knees. Careful not to injure the shoots themselves, she tugged at the weeds that somehow had failed to choke them.

Footsteps sounded on the path. She didn't look up until she heard Inez Ramirez's voice.

"I brought you some iced tea. I see I should have brought the sunscreen. What are you doing, besides getting sunburned and dirty?"

Amber opened her mouth, but the longtime Colton housekeeper rushed on, as she always did.

"You are supposed to be relaxing. You're on vacation."

"I'm too restless to relax."

"Your swim failed to help?"

Amber shrugged. Swimming alone wasn't much fun, and it certainly wasn't stimulating. She swept a hand toward the far corner of the courtyard. "Remember how beautiful the garden looked, Inez, back when my mother loved to tend it?" She didn't say, "back when she loved to tend us all," but she could tell from the look on Inez's pretty, expressive face that she was thinking the same thing.

Inez didn't believe in feeling sorry for herself, and she didn't allow those around her to wallow in self-pity, either. Placing her hands on hips that had rounded over the years, she lowered her chin and raised her eyebrows. "If you would get serious about finding a husband and having babies, you would be too tired to be bored."

Amber rubbed the dirt from her hands then brushed a blade of grass off her thigh. Finding a man and making babies was Inez's answer to every problem. "Men are after two things, Inez: Sex and money, not necessarily in that order."

Inez crossed herself, her lips moving in silent prayer. Amber couldn't be certain whether she did it for Inez and Marco's two beautiful daughters, Maya, who had recently had a beautiful baby girl, and Lana, who had been distracted lately, or for Amber. "Not all men," she said when her litany was completed.

Amber reached for another weed. "Name one."

"My Marco. And your father and brothers are good men."

Amber shook her head. "Okay. Now name one man who fits that description and also isn't married or related to me."

As far as Amber was concerned, Inez's silence spoke volumes. Recalling the sound she'd heard a while ago when a car had pulled into the driveway on the other side of the sprawling estate, she asked, "Who's here, Inez?"

If she'd been looking, she might have noticed the change that had come over the older woman's features. She certainly would have seen the sudden glint in those dark brown eyes and been suspicious of the way the wheels suddenly seemed to start turning behind them.

"Oh," Inez said casually, "someone to see your father."

Before Amber could question further, the older woman was hurrying toward the wide French doors that led into the house. Sighing again, Amber turned her attention back to the weeds.

Tripp Calhoun's footsteps echoed on the gleaming tile floors inside the Coltons' spacious home, the sound changing to a muted thud as he stepped onto a richly colored rug. He stopped before a massive stone fireplace and viewed the leather sofas and large armoire that undoubtedly cost more than he made in a month. Not a thing was out of place in the entire room—except maybe him.

Memories had washed over him when he'd pulled through the wrought-iron gates leading to Joe and Meredith Colton's estate. He'd been fifteen when he'd first set foot on the grounds, angry, rebellious and scared to death, though he'd hidden the fear well, the way he'd learned to hide most emotions back then.

Meredith Colton had seen right through him. To this day, he didn't know how she'd done it.

He fiddled with the clasp on his watch, slipped the band over his hand. Starting to pace again, he looped the watch over a finger and twirled it in a nervous gesture. He didn't remember the room being so austere. Hell, he could have been looking at a picture in one of the dog-eared magazines in his waiting room.

They called this place Hacienda de Alegria. House of Joy. There didn't appear to be much joy in it anymore.

Tripp hadn't been back often over the years. It wasn't as if he'd been one of Joe and Meredith's real kids, or even one of their adopted children. He'd been a foster child. Not that he wasn't thankful. Joe and Meredith had saved him from the streets of L.A., given him a home for one life-altering summer. Where he was today and who he'd become was due to their influence. They'd put up a good share of the money for college and med school. Tripp owed them, big-time and he'd worked his tail off to make them proud.

Pausing at a marble-topped table, he picked up a photograph. The two young boys in the picture looked to be about eight and ten. They were the youngest Colton children. He'd only seen them a couple of times, so it wasn't surprising that they didn't look familiar. Their mother, Meredith Colton sure should have looked more familiar, though. And yet, she didn't. Oh, she was as beautiful as ever, but the image he'd carried in his mind of the woman who'd taken him in was in sharp contrast to the cool, brittle woman in the photograph. Something had happened to this family years ago, and no one had been able to fix it.

The heavy thud of footsteps behind him drew him around. Inez Ramirez smiled as she approached, muttering that Joe was going to be tied up on the phone for some time yet. Tripp expected Inez to suggest he come back another time. Instead, she bustled over, retrieved the photograph from his hand, and, returning it to the table, said, "Everyone is fidgety today. Go. Wait out by the pool. Get some sun and fresh air."

Inez had aged during the seventeen years since Tripp had stayed here. Her black hair now had a wide streak of gray that started at her forehead and disappeared in the bun at her nape. She ushered him through the living room and into the courtyard. "You wait out there. You relax."

She was still as bossy as ever.

"I'm thirty-two years old, Inez. Not six."

"Thirty-two is a good age, I think."

"A good age for what?"

Her smile was smug. It put him on edge, because a smile like that always meant that a woman had something up her sleeve.

She slapped something into his hand. "A good age to feel young. Enjoy the sunshine." With that, she turned on her heel and disappeared.

Tripp knew better than to argue with a woman like Inez Ramirez. And he wanted to talk to Joe. He supposed he could wait out here as well as inside.

The hand he smoothed over his shirt did little to erase the wrinkles it'd gotten as a result of the hour of sleep he'd caught at the hospital. Wandering to a table near the pool, he noticed a tray containing glasses and a tall pitcher of iced tea. Next, he caught a movement out of the corner of his eye. Well, well, well. He wasn't alone in the courtyard.

One woman appeared to be sleeping, fully clothed, on a chaise lounge on the other side of the pool. Another woman clad in a pale lavender swimsuit was on all fours near the center of the garden. He couldn't see her face, but this angle awarded him a view of long legs and the nicest rear end he'd seen in a long time.

"Lose something?" he called.

The woman swung around in surprise. Shading her

eyes with one hand, a smile spread slowly across her face. "Why, Tripp Calhoun! I didn't know you were here."

"Amber Colton. It's been a while."

She placed a finger to her lips. "Shh. Claire's sleeping."

He cast a cursory glance at the other woman, who hadn't so much as moved a muscle, then walked a little closer to Amber. From this position he could see the tan line along the inner swells of her breasts. It wasn't easy not to stare. She certainly had curves in all the right places. Her hips flared just enough to entice a man's imagination and her legs were long.

"You're probably thinking I remind you of my mother."

His eyebrows arched before he could stop them. That wasn't what he'd been thinking at all. "I don't recall ever seeing your mother pull weeds wearing a purple bikini."

As if she was suddenly aware of the view she was inadvertently awarding him, she rose almost shyly to her feet. Amber Colton, shy?

She glanced at the bottle of sunscreen in his hand. "Did Inez send you out with that?"

Inez. Ah. So this was what she'd had up her sleeve. "That woman is trying to start something."

"With you?" Amber asked.

He nodded.

No, Amber Colton definitely wasn't shy. She *was* very blond, extremely pretty. He'd wondered how tall she was. Now that she was standing he'd put her at close to five-six. A leggy five-six.

He jerked his gaze away before he got caught looking. "Very funny. Obviously, Inez doesn't know that I'm not the type to have a tête-à-tête with a rich little heiress out by the mansion's pool.''

A blind man would have caught the haughty lift of Amber's chin. Tripp figured he probably deserved the scathing comment that was certain to follow. After all, he hadn't exactly been nice. Truthful, but not nice.

There was a terse silence. But the scathing comment never came. She didn't accept the bottle of sunscreen from his outstretched hand, either. Instead, she strolled to an ornate bench and reached for a white cover-up. When she'd fastened the last big button, she said, ''I still say your name should be Chip, not Tripp, to go with the mountain-sized chip you carry around your shoulder.''

They stared at each other, unmoving.

A memory swirled over Tripp, and he smiled, a rarity for him. ''That was the first thing you said to me the summer I stayed here.'' She'd been what, nine or ten? That would make her twenty-six or seven now. ''You've grown up, Amber.''

Amber found herself gazing into Tripp's dark brown eyes, and wondering… Oh, no she didn't. After that last comment of his, she wasn't about to give in to the curious swooping sensation tugging at her insides.

Stark and white, his smile did crazy things to her heart rate. She dragged her gaze away. It was bad enough that his look sent a tingling to the pit of her stomach. She would be darned if she would let him know it.

She remembered the first time she saw him. He'd been fifteen, lean and belligerent and street-smart. He was still lean today, but his shoulders were wider, his chest thicker. His jet-black hair wasn't as long as hers anymore, but it was still too long to be considered reputable. There was more than a hint of Latino in his features, passed on to him from one of his grandfathers, who had immigrated

to America when still a boy. The first time she'd laid
eyes on Tripp, she'd thought he looked like Zorro, the
legendary superhero her brothers used to pretend to be
when they were kids.

With his looks, he could have acted on one of those
medical dramas or police-detective shows. Tripp was a
pediatrician now. Her gaze caught on the gold stud in his
ear; he certainly didn't look like the pediatricians she'd
visited as a child.

The good manners and etiquette instilled in her from
the cradle dictated that she stride to the table and pour
iced tea into the waiting crystal glasses. His fingers
brushed hers as he accepted the glass. Their gazes met,
held. For a moment, neither of them moved.

That tingling was back in the pit of her stomach,
stronger than ever. She didn't know why she glanced at
his knuckles. His hands were large, his fingers long, his
knuckles bony, especially the first two. She reached out
with her other hand, covering the hard ridge of the largest
one with her finger. "So these broken bones healed."

He drew his hand away from hers very slowly and took
a sip from the glass. Ice jangled, his Adam's apple bob-
bled slightly as he swallowed. A bead of perspiration
trailed down his neck, disappearing beneath the collar of
his white dress shirt. He seemed nervous.

Or was it something else?

Running a hand through his hair, he peered into the
courtyard and said, "I was sure your parents were going
to send me to another foster home before I even unpacked
my bags."

Amber decided she must have been imagining his unease. "You said Peter Bradenton threw the first punch."

"I lied."

"I know."

He spun around. "You knew?"

She'd never heard more surprise or disbelief in two little words. He wasn't smiling now, and yet something was still happening to her, something delicious and exciting and fun.

He said, "How long have you known?"

"I saw the fight from my bedroom window."

Tripp was looking at her, his expression one of total dismay.

"Then why didn't you tell your father the truth?"

She sashayed closer. "If I'd done that, you wouldn't have spent all these years trying to make it up to him. Guilt is a great motivator. Besides, he knew."

"You just said you didn't tell him."

She pulled a face. "I didn't have to. He always knew when any of us lied. Besides, Peter Bradenton had it coming. He was always trying to put people in their places. In your place wasn't where you wanted to be."

"You were what, nine years old, and you knew that?"

She batted her eyelashes. "Girls mature faster than boys." She watched in fascination as his lips parted and his eyes went from very wide to narrow slits. He wasn't immune to her charms. He looked as surprised about that as she was.

She remembered the fight between Tripp and Peter Bradenton, and the chaos it caused. The Colton rule was: No fighting. Period. They could argue all they wanted, and had, but her parents simply did not allow fighting. Tripp was the only foster child to come through the ranks who broke the rule. And he did it the first week he was here. Her mother had heard the commotion and had come running. Without saying a word, she'd separated them. Still silent, she'd gotten Peter a towel for his bleeding nose, and Tripp an icepack for his hand. She sent Peter home, and Tripp to the stables to tell Joe. Amber had followed from a distance. When her dad had confronted Tripp about lying, she'd slunk out of the shadows and backed up Tripp's story, saying that Peter took the first swing. She'd shaken beneath her father's probing stare. In the end, he'd told Tripp to have Meredith take him to the doctor for X rays, and then sent them both back up to the house.

Tripp hadn't said a word until they were well away from the stables. She'd expected a thank-you. Instead, he'd shoved his hair behind his ears, his lips curling with contempt as he said, "I don't need anybody doing me any favors, least of all a scrawny, spoiled little rich girl like you."

She'd stuck her nose in the air and informed him that his name should have been Chip, not Tripp. He'd stared at her, and she'd held his gaze despite the fact that she was half his size. Back then she hadn't known they were rich and she wasn't spoiled, no matter what he said. Even then she'd known what really mattered, and it wasn't something a person could buy. What truly mattered was trust, love and loyalty. Everything else faded away without them.

Amber looked around the courtyard today. The garden, with all its demanding tea roses and ornamental shrubs and bushes had faded, too, as if it too was lacking what it truly needed.

"What have you been doing out here?"

His question brought her back to their earlier conversation. Swirling the iced tea she had yet to taste, she said, "I went for a swim. Then I watched the clouds."

"You watch clouds? Like a meteorologist?"

She shook her head. "Nothing that interesting. It was a game we used to play when we were kids."

Tripp looked around the garden, with its pool and fountain and women with nothing better to do than stretch out and catch a nap. Places like this were made for lounging. He didn't have enough hours in a day to accomplish everything he needed to do, let alone the time to watch clouds and play games. Or wait, for that matter. His receptionist liked to say that Tripp became a doctor because it enabled him to be the one keeping others waiting, instead of the other way around.

He glanced at the house where he was supposed to meet with Joe. Maybe Tripp wasn't the most patient man on the planet, but the real reason he'd become a pediatrician was tied up with this house, and the people who'd taken him in all those years ago.

"Want to try?" Amber asked.

He looked at her blankly. "Try what?"

"See that cloud over there?"

He peered at the horizon. He saw a lot of clouds. "Which one?"

"The one shaped like Smoky the Bear."

He squinted at the distant sky. The description didn't help.

"Look."

He was looking, dammit.

"There. To the right of the line formed by a jet's exhaust."

Tilting his head at an angle to match hers, he said, "That tall cloud over there?"

"Yes." She sounded breathless. "Do you see it? The one that looks like Smoky the Bear?"

He looked down at her, and forgot what he'd been doing. Her eyes were green, her lashes long. Her hair was mussed, a riot of golden tangles around her face and neck. Her mouth was pretty, her lips full and slightly pouty. Heat stirred inside him. He was tempted to kiss her, here and now. As a gust of wind fluttered her soft white beach cover-up, pressing it against her body, the heat moved lower.

"A bear?" He cleared his throat. What the hell had happened to his voice? Forcing his eyes back to the clouds, he said, "I don't see any bear. Joe DiMaggio, maybe."

He was vaguely aware that she'd eased closer. He misjudged just how close; the next time he moved, his arm brushed something incredibly soft. He glanced down again and stepped back as if he'd touched fire.

His beeper sounded and he jumped again. This time he swore under his breath, and reached for the pager. Reading the display, he said, "I need to call the hospital in Ukiah."

She motioned to the cordless lying on a low table, then watched as he picked it up. After punching several numbers, he spoke in low tones. Replacing the phone to the table, he said, "I have to meet a patient at the hospital in Ukiah."

He was halfway to the house when she called, "What do you want me to tell my father?"

He turned around. Amber wished she were close enough to get a good look at the expression in his dark brown eyes.

"Tell him I'll call him later."

"I'll tell him. It was good to see you again, Tripp."

"You, too."

She smiled. As if it required a conscious effort, he broke eye contact and slowly resumed his retreat. Rather than leave via the house, he changed directions, veering toward the side yard. Less than a minute later, she heard his car start on the other side of the house.

What in the world had just happened?

She stared at her iced tea. Closing her eyes, she placed the cold glass against her forehead.

She'd reacted to the sight and sound and touch of Tripp Calhoun. And he'd reacted to her. She couldn't remember the last time she'd felt so breathless without doing a thing. Her entire body felt sensitized. If she were to jump in the pool right now, she would sizzle all over.

A door opened, and Inez bustled outside. "Your father is off the phone." The other woman looked all around. "Where's Tripp?"

Amber's vision remained fixed on the path Tripp had taken. "Something came up. An emergency at the hospital. He had to leave."

Inez made no reply.

Amber could feel Inez's penetrating gaze. "What is it?" Amber asked.

Turning her hand over, Inez said, "He left his watch inside. Did he say when he will return?"

"No. I'm afraid he didn't." Amber reached for the watch. "I'll be sure he gets it, Inez."

"That is a good idea, I think." Inez turned away before Amber could decide what to make of the dark-haired woman's beaming smile.

Amber strode to the shaded side of the pool. Bending down, she gently shook her friend. "Claire, wake up."

A pair of baby-blue eyes fluttered open. "I don't want to wake up. I was dreaming about this amazing, ruggedly attractive, dark-haired man."

Amber smiled. "It wasn't a dream, Claire. Believe me. Come on. I have to go to Ukiah."

Claire sat up languidly. "Ukiah, really?" she said, pushing her straight, coffee-colored hair away from her face. "Could you drop me off at the gallery first? You can fill me in on the way."

Half an hour later Amber pulled her car into the alley behind Claire's art gallery in Prosperino. Claire opened her door and climbed out, then leaned down to say good-bye through the open window. Behind her, Amber noticed a door opening on the second story of a building in the distance. Something about the woman descending the stairs seemed familiar. Very familiar.

"Amber, is something wrong?" Claire asked.

Amber didn't take her eyes off the woman, whose hair was hidden beneath a scarf, her eyes behind dark glasses, until she'd disappeared around the corner. "I thought I just saw my mother."

Claire turned to look behind her, but the woman was gone. "Your mother, here?" Claire asked incredulously.

"I know." Amber couldn't imagine her mother lowering herself enough to visit the art district of Prosperino. It must have been somebody else. For the sake of curiosity, she pointed to the building in the distance. "Is that a business or an apartment?"

Claire shuddered. "I guess you could call it a business. A shady private investigator rents the upstairs office. I can imagine your mother there as easily as I can imagine her strolling the streets in the red-light district."

"Prosperino doesn't have a red-light district."

"I'm thinking about starting one."

"Claire."

Claire winked. "Now, don't you have someplace to go and some ruggedly attractive man to see?"

Amber shook her head, nodded, and finally smiled. While Claire strolled into the second of the two art studios she'd opened a few months ago, Amber put her car in gear.

The engine purred like a contented tiger. Her mother had given her the shiny little sports car for her last birthday. It was red. She didn't even like red. Before the car accident, Meredith Colton had known that.

What would her mother have been doing visiting a shady private investigator in Prosperino, when she'd made such a point these past ten years of finding fault with everything about the town? It must have been someone else.

Amber glanced at the sky. The clouds had thinned, forming a haze, the one shaped like Smoky the Bear blurring with all the others. Joe Dimaggio, indeed. Tripp's smile, stark and white, shimmered across her mind.

What was it with men and baseball players?

Her last boyfriend had been a Giants fan. He'd enjoyed using baseball metaphors to describe their relationship. He'd spent the biggest share of their dates trying to get past first base. The night he'd presented her with a three-carat diamond, he'd expected a grand-slam home run. The ring had been pretty, but it wasn't home run material. And neither was he. She'd turned down his proposal. Last she'd heard he was pursuing some other rich girl down in San Francisco.

Amber thought about Tripp. Until his arm had brushed the outer swell of her breast, she'd thought she was the only one aware of the attraction between them. Gracious, he probably wasn't even admitting that he'd felt any such thing.

Whether he admitted it or not, she knew he had.

She touched the watch in her pocket and smiled. This was better than a vacation.

She wasn't bored anymore.

TWO

A blast of hot air hit Amber the moment she opened her car door. Taking a deep breath, she placed a steadying hand on her queasy stomach and climbed slowly to her feet. It had been cool and foggy along the coast when she'd left Prosperino, which just went to show that the locals were right. There really were three seasons in this part of California, often all in the same day.

She rotated a kink from between her shoulder blades then stepped away from her car. The drive to Ukiah seemed like forever. Though it was only forty-five miles, it was like her father always said: "Prosperino is near a lot of places, but you can't get there from here." Joe Colton compensated by flying whenever possible. Not Amber. She'd reached the brink of motion sickness negotiating the twenty-five mile stretch of Highway 101 that wound around cliffs and up and down hills over the coastal mountains. Flying would have done her in. Thank goodness the road that ran north and south on this side of the mountains was straighter and mostly four-lane.

She took a shaky step, popped a breath mint into her mouth and peeled off her jacket. So this, she thought as she looked around, her heels clicking over the paved parking lot, was where Tripp worked. He was going to be so surprised to see her.

The streets of Ukiah were lined with beautiful old Victorian houses. The sprawling hospital was old, too, but it looked as if it had been remodeled in recent years. Double doors slid open as she approached the building. Folding her jacket over one arm, she peered around the lobby trying to decide where to go from here.

Across the waiting room, a short, heavyset nurse with broad shoulders and a hairstyle that resembled an army helmet stood behind a high counter.

"Hello," Amber said, sauntering closer.

Clutching a pen between thick fingers, the gray-haired nurse looked at Amber over the tops of the reading glasses perched low on her broad nose. "May I help you?"

Amber put on her friendliest smile. "I'd like to see Dr. Calhoun."

The only things that moved on the stern-faced nurse were the brown eyes giving Amber a thorough once-over. "He isn't taking appointments this afternoon."

Amber eased closer and smiled conspiratorially. "That's okay. I don't have an appointment."

She knew the blunder for what it was the second it was out. Nurse Proctor—that was what her name badge said—turned her attention back to the chart. Amber was dismissed.

Obviously, Nurse Proctor didn't know that Amber

wasn't easily dismissed. "I won't take up much of his time," she said, trying on an even bigger smile.

The nurse's eyes remained fixed on the chart.

Amber tried another tack. "I know he's here because he told me he was coming here in answer to an emergency call."

"In that case you'll understand why he can't be disturbed."

Amber didn't expect to pull him away from an emergency. That call had come hours ago. If he was still busy, fine. If not, what harm could there be in allowing her a moment or two to see him?

"Is Tripp still in the building?"

The nurse made a noncommittal reply without opening her mouth. Recognizing an impenetrable brick wall when she crashed into one, Amber moved away from the counter, as far out of range of Nurse Proctor's peripheral vision as possible. She pretended a keen interest in her chipped manicure.

The elevator dinged. The door opened, and a young man clad in green scrubs ambled into the lobby.

"There you are, Fred!" The no-nonsense nurse motioned him to the desk. "They're waiting for these charts up in OB."

With the jaunty walk of a guy who knew he looked good both coming and going, Fred took the charts and started back toward the elevator. Just then, a woman ran in from outside, yelling, "Somebody, help. I think my daughter's ankle is broken!"

Nurse Proctor rushed around the counter, grabbed a wheelchair and bustled toward the sliding doors. Amber slipped quietly into the elevator behind Fred.

He punched a button. Leaving his hand hovering over the panel, he asked, "What floor?"

She had no idea, but she said, "Three, I guess."

Brown eyes twinkled as he looked her up and down. "Looks like you're going my way."

The door closed and the elevator slowly started to climb. Amber placed a hand to her stomach.

"Are you afraid of heights?" he asked.

She smiled wanly. "I get motion sick easily."

With a lift of his sandy-blond eyebrows, he grinned, his smile white and just crooked enough to look beguiling. "My sister swears by the ear patch. You need someone to take your mind off it. Lucky for you I'm here." He looked her in the eye and smiled again. "My shift is almost over. We could grab a cup of coffee or a bite to eat or whatever..." His voice trailed off suggestively.

The elevator continued to climb. "Look, Fred—"

"Fredrico."

"But the nurse called you—"

"Proctor calls me a lot of things. Trust me."

"Fredrico, I'm afraid there's an age requirement any man I see must meet."

He eased closer. For a boy, he certainly knew his moves. "How old would I have to be?"

"Old enough to vote."

"Too bad. You're missing a great opportunity. If it's true that men reach their sexual prime at seventeen, I hit that mark a mere two years ago. I may not be old enough to vote, but I can personally guarantee you that I haven't even started to go downhill."

The elevator glided to a stop on the second floor. Leaning against the rail, Amber said, "You don't say."

"I could prove it, if you'd like."

She held up one hand. "We'll just consider it my loss. Could you tell me where I might find Dr. Calhoun?"

"If you'll tell me your phone number, we'll make it an even exchange."

While Amber was chuckling, the door opened and a woman pushing a cumbersome cart got in. The door closed, taking the three occupants up to the next floor. The lady with the cart got off, and Fredrico said, "I know where Doc Calhoun is."

"You do?"

"I'll take you there, but you have to promise not to tell Proctor."

Amber grinned up at the sandy-haired young man. She'd felt strangely carefree ever since she'd talked to Tripp out in the garden, and she just couldn't help responding to the secrecy in Fredrico's expression. "Okay. I promise."

"He's with a patient. This way."

They got off the elevator and strode through doors bearing a sign for authorized personnel only.

At first, she couldn't place the sound coming from someplace up ahead. Then it came again. Rounding a corner, she whispered, "Are dogs allowed in this hospital?"

With a shake of his head, Fredrico pointed to a room up ahead. "It's a little unconventional. Proctor can't find out. There's Doc Calhoun. See the little kid he's with? His name's P.J."

Amber crept closer on tiptoe. Tripp was sitting on the edge of a bed, in a room at the end of the hall. Nestled in one arm was a pudgy tan puppy. A little boy with curly brown hair, a bandage on the side of his head and a cast on one arm stared straight ahead.

"What's wrong with him?" Amber whispered.

"He got banged up pretty bad, but mostly he's mad. He's four years old and he wants his mama."

"Where is she?"

"She died in the accident."

Both of Amber's hands came up, covering her mouth. "What about his father?"

"Nobody knows where he is. P.J.'s been here a week. There's a good chance he'll be okay, but his arm got cut up, and he's gonna have to work to get full use back. He hasn't exactly been responsive or cooperative. Yesterday Doc Calhoun noticed him watching a television show about a dog. And my girlfriend's dog had a litter of pups, and well..."

Amber's eyebrows raised a fraction. "Your girlfriend?"

Fredrico started to nod. Realizing his faux pas, he simply shrugged.

The puppy yipped again. All at once it wiggled out of Tripp's hands, landing in the boy's lap. The little boy looked down dazedly. And then, as if in slow motion, he reached out, tentatively touching the puppy's fur. It was all the invitation the dog needed. Tail wagging, the pudgy little puppy licked P.J.'s face. P.J. blinked, smiled and let loose a belly laugh.

"Folks sure are gonna miss that man around here."

Amber cast a questioning look at Fredrico, but he was already starting to move away from her and didn't see. "If I don't get these charts over to OB, Proctor'll send out a search party. If she hasn't already."

Amber whispered, "Goodbye, then, and thanks." Her gaze returned to the man and child in the room up ahead. Tripp was so engrossed in the boy, he didn't seem to know she was watching. Her breath caught just below the little hollow at the base of her throat. With his stubby ponytail and earring, he still looked like the street-smart kid he'd been years ago. She was beginning to realize that he was so much more than that.

His voice was a low murmur, his touch gentle as he showed P.J. how to pet the puppy. Mesmerized, Amber acknowledged the fact that this wasn't simply a case of no longer being bored. This was something else, something she couldn't name but wanted to explore.

Tripp chose that moment to glance into the hall. Their gazes locked, and awareness fluttered around the walls of her chest. He didn't smile, but she felt the heat in his gaze just the same.

P.J. said something, and Tripp turned his attention back to the boy. Shaken, and touched, Amber smoothed her hands down her slacks, her fingers tracing the outline of the watch in her pocket. Her heart beat wildly. Unwilling to intrude on the doctor-patient moment, she wrenched herself away, and retraced her footsteps to the elevator.

What was happening to her?

She wanted more than ever to talk to Tripp. She considered waiting in the lobby, but the thought of being scrutinized by Nurse Proctor was less than appealing. If only she had something more constructive to do here.

She looked around. Some people hated hospitals. Not Amber. She dealt with them on a weekly basis in her work for the Hopechest Foundation, an organization her mother had founded years ago. Today, the foundation funded centers for children in need all across the country. Among them were day-care centers for children who were HIV positive, and after-school programs, and sporting events for city kids confined to housing projects.

Amber looked around again, recalling the children she'd seen working in the fields during her drive from

Prosperino. Needy kids weren't confined to housing projects or large cities. They were everywhere.

Striding to the nurse's station she'd passed earlier, she introduced herself. At her mention of her affiliation with the Hopechest Foundation, the other woman was all ears.

"I was wondering if you might direct me to the person in charge of special programs to help children in need."

The young nurse beamed her approval. "Directions won't do. I'll take you there myself."

Now this, Amber thought, was more like it. By the time she left the hospital administrator's office, the scent of hospital food wafted on the air. The meeting had taken longer than she'd expected. Wondering if Tripp was still in the building, she followed the exit signs through a labyrinth of hallways. She must have taken a wrong turn, because she didn't recognize this wing. Sure enough, she came to the stairs, not the elevators.

Pausing to get her bearings, she turned and started back the way she'd come. She'd taken only three steps when the low murmur of voices carried to her ears from an open door a few feet away.

"People around here are going to miss you, Calhoun."

She stopped in her tracks. People were going to miss Tripp? Now that she thought about it, Fredrico had implied the same thing. Where was Tripp going?

She turned again. Striding to the door, she raised her hand, prepared to knock. The voices started again, and Amber's hand remained suspended in midair.

"But if you insist on leaving, I'm putting dibs on your office."

Tripp looked at the man sitting on the other side of his desk. Aside from their chosen professions and their affiliation with this hospital, he and Gavin Cooper were complete opposites and unlikely friends. With his blond hair and blue eyes, Coop looked more like a beach bum than a brilliant doctor. He was laid-back and easygoing. Dubbed the Don Juan of County General, he wore the perpetual, slightly bedraggled, contented look of a man who'd recently crawled out of a woman's bed. Even now, slouched in a chair, his arms folded, his feet on Tripp's desk, ankles crossed, he made a science out of relaxing.

Not Tripp.

He shot out of his chair, slid his hands into his pockets and jangled his keys. "I haven't gotten the position yet, Coop."

He found himself standing at his window, his back to his friend. He had a great view of the mountains from here. It wasn't the Mendocino Ridges that drew his gaze, but the parking lot below. The lot contained the usual assortment of vans and family sedans. The candy-apple-red Porsche stuck out like a sore thumb. He'd seen that vehicle parked in the driveway at Hacienda de Alegria that very afternoon.

It belonged to Amber Colton.

When he'd happened to glance into the hall outside P.J.'s room an hour ago, he'd thought he was seeing things. Amber had stood so still, she could have been a mirage, and he, a thirsty man in the desert.

Her hair had been long and loose around her tanned shoulders, her body, lean and svelte beneath formfitting slacks. A bolt of sexual attraction had come out of nowhere. If he hadn't been sitting down, it would have knocked him off his feet. He couldn't afford that kind of attraction. He'd already been down that road once: The poor street kid made good and the bored, rich heiress. It hadn't been pretty.

"It's only a matter of time. After all, who better than you…" Coop's voice droned on in the background.

Tripp ran a hand down his face, scrubbing it over the stubble on his jaw and on down the front of his wrinkled shirt. That red sports car in the parking lot was no mirage. What was Amber doing at County General?

"Calhoun, are you even listening?"

"I heard you. It so happens I received a letter from Montgomery Perkins in Santa Rosa yesterday. The field has been narrowed to two."

"Who's your contender? Anybody I know?"

His back to Coop, Tripp said, "Does the name Spencer ring a bell?"

"First or last?"

"Last."

"Spencer? As in, Derek Spencer?"

The next time Tripp looked, Coop was sitting up straighter.

"The one and only."

A succinct and unbecoming but fitting word spewed out of Cooper's mouth about the same time his feet hit the floor. "I still can't believe he became a pediatrician. I always figured Spencer for the type to specialize in plastic surgery, not so he could repair cleft palates and facial scars, but so he could do nose jobs and boob implants for wannabe starlets down in Hollywood. What would he want with a position in a private practice in Santa Rosa?"

"It gets worse."

"How could it get any worse than competing with your backstabbing rival from med school?"

"It seems Derek's gotten himself engaged."

"Who's the unlucky woman?"

Any other time, Tripp would have appreciated his friend's sarcasm. "Olivia."

"Your Olivia?"

Tripp didn't bother to remind Coop that Olivia wasn't his anymore, if she ever had been. Olivia Babcock's father was an influential man in the medical field, capable of pulling very impressive strings. It didn't look good for Tripp. It didn't look good at all.

"Does this mean I won't be getting first dibs on this office?" Coop asked.

"I'm not giving up that easily."

"Yeah? In that case, listen up. People don't mind if an E.R. doctor is a player, but parents like their kids' pediatricians to be family men, so if I were you, I'd find myself a woman with a couple of kids. Better yet, find one with relatives as influential as Olivia's, too. Stat."

Tripp was in the process of scowling when he heard a noise in the hallway outside his office door. He caught a whiff of expensive, exotic perfume a millisecond before Amber Colton breezed in. There wasn't a wrinkle in her sage-green pantsuit. He didn't know how rich people did that.

Tripp wasn't surprised at the change that came over Coop. The man went on testosterone alert every time a woman came within ten yards of him. But Amber wasn't paying him any attention. She was looking at Tripp.

"Hello," she murmured, her voice just sultry enough to sound seductive. Reaching into her pocket, she drew out his watch. Easing closer, she said, "I thought you might want this back before tonight."

She had to know how that sounded. Glancing over her shoulder, she smiled at Coop and said, "Does he leave his things lying around the hospital, too?"

Tripp had to force his gaping mouth shut.

Amber appeared completely nonplussed. With a flutter of eyelashes and the sureness that the rich seemed to be born with, she extended her hand toward Coop. "Hello. I'm Amber Colton."

Coop's voice lowered, softened, mellowed. "Gavin Cooper, head of E.R. Colton? Any relation to Joseph Colton?"

"You know my father?"

Coop chuckled. "Not personally." Rising languidly to his feet, he released Amber's hand. He looked Tripp in the eye and said, "I underestimated you, my friend. I see you're already on it. You show up at that dinner party this weekend with a woman like Amber on your arm, and you'll be a shoe-in for the position in Santa Rosa. At the very least you'll give good old Spencer a run for his money. I'll leave you two alone."

Still grinning, Coop left, closing the door behind him.

Amber stared up at Tripp. The room, all at once, was very quiet. Maybe too quiet. Something was wrong.

Tripp's eyes had narrowed. Hers were wide open. His breathing was deep, hers, shallow. In the tight space so near him, she thought of a dozen questions. What position? What does it have to do with Santa Rosa? What rival? Who was Olivia?

Three separate times, she opened her mouth to voice one of them. Her gaze caught on Tripp's mouth. He really had a marvelous mouth, the bottom lip fuller than the top. Right now, both were set in a straight line.

"Is something wrong?"

The question seemed to bring him to his senses. He took a deep breath, let it all out and paced to the other side of the cluttered office. "Coop thinks we're lovers. What on earth could possibly be wrong? And what are you doing here, besides charming the socks off every male you meet?''

Amber recognized an attack when she was under one. She didn't understand the reason for it. "I repeat. What's wrong?"

"Nothing."

"Bull."

That got his attention. "Do you make a habit of eavesdropping?"

"The door was open," she said quietly.

He glanced over her shoulder, and so did she. The door was closed now. And they were alone. Tripp took a backward step, putting more distance between them.

"Coop can hold his own," he said, "but the orderly I saw you with earlier is still a boy. It was like watching the bored, pampered house cat play with a poor defenseless mouse."

Poor defenseless mouse? For long seconds, Amber could only stare at him, stunned. Finally, she said, "Fredrico is about as defenseless as an octopus."

"Fredrico?"

She'd been prepared for several questions. That wasn't one of them. "He helped you smuggle that puppy into the hospital. Surely you know his name."

"I know Fred's name. Everybody does."

She was getting a bad feeling about this. Now that she thought about it, Nurse Proctor had called the boy Fred. "I see."

Tripp was on a roll. "Good, because Don and Mary Smith might have named their son Frederick, but definitely not Fredrico."

All right, already. The boy had pulled one over on her. That didn't explain the reason for Tripp's bad mood, or

what he and Cooper had been talking about. "Let's talk
about positions, shall we?"

Tripp's pulses leapt. "I beg your pardon?"

"Didn't I overhear something about a position you're
hoping to gain down in Santa Rosa?"

Ah. She was referring to the position he'd applied for
at an exclusive, private practice in Santa Rosa, not, er,
the position for another activity completely unrelated to
medicine. He cleared his throat. Clearing his mind of the
mental picture that had sprung straight out of his imagination was more difficult to accomplish.

"There's an opening in pediatrics there. The practice
is affiliated with the oldest, most prestigious hospital in
Santa Rosa. It's larger than Ukiah County General, and
wealthier by far. I would receive a higher salary, and
ultimately, I could reach a lot more kids."

"Then I don't see the problem. I'll do it."

She stared up at him with luminous green eyes so large
it was easy to get lost in their depths. "What exactly are
you proposing?"

He didn't have much mind capacity left at this point,
but even he had enough to appreciate the effort she put
forth to keep from rolling her eyes. "Your rival is going
to be there with his fiancée, right? I'll go with you. Then
you and your rival will be starting on even ground."

He stared at her for several seconds. She looked happy,
as if she was enjoying herself. Again, he thought of a
pampered house cat. Olivia used to look like that, too. It
was a sobering thought.

"What are you doing here, Amber?"

Her eyes delved into his. She really had very expressive eyes. He imagined they would look this way, large
and luminous, in the dark. Whoa. That kind of thinking

could be dangerous to a man who was trying to keep his wits about him.

She reached out, touching the watch she'd placed in his hand minutes earlier. "Inez discovered this in the living room at Hacienda de Alegria. You were right. About Inez, I mean. She was matchmaking, just as you said. It would have been apparent even without all the advice she gave me along with directions to the hospital here in Ukiah. Don't worry. I have no intention of allowing Inez to manipulate me."

It was true, Amber thought. She didn't allow many people to push her around. Besides, she didn't need anybody to play matchmaker for her. The three marriage proposals she'd received these past five years spoke for themselves. Amber Colton knew how to get a man. She was beginning to doubt she would ever find one to love, however. There *had* been a strong attraction between her and Tripp in the garden earlier that day. Though it wasn't love, it had been fun.

"You want this position. I'd like to help you get it."

"What's in it for you?" he asked.

"What makes you think there has to be something in it for me?"

The sound he made in the back of his throat spoke volumes. There was arrogance and belligerence in the lift of that chiseled chin. In that instant, he reminded her of how he'd looked after she'd stood up for him to her father all those years ago.

"All right," she said. "We were friends when we were kids. I'm hoping we can be friends again. Friends help each other. If acting as your fiancée for one evening helps you gain a position you want, so be it."

"I don't like lying. Lies are like dogs. They seem

harmless to your face, but the minute you turn your back, they go straight for the seat of your pants.''

''Pretending isn't the same as lying. If you need—''

He shook his head. "I want to do this on my own, without the help of a bored heiress in need of a project.''

Her mouth fell open. She snapped it closed. Finally she said, "Of all the condescending...'' But words failed her. She swung around in a huff and reached the door in three brisk strides. "If you ever decide to come down off your high horse, give me a call.''

She slammed the door.

She hadn't gone far when she heard Tripp being paged to the ICU.

He reached the elevator seconds after her. They entered in single file. She punched the button for the lobby, he the second floor.

When the door closed, he said, "I suppose I owe you an apology.''

She stared straight ahead. "That didn't sound very convincing, Tripp. Unless you're sincere, forget it.''

They rode in silence.

"If you'll excuse me,'' he said when the elevator stopped on two.

She stepped aside without comment.

He started to get off, then paused in midstride. Finally, he resumed his exit.

He turned around to look at her just as the door began to close. She stared at him for a moment, then looked away. An instant later, the door closed and the elevator jerked into motion.

Friends? she thought clutching the rail.

Ha! She'd received friendlier goodbyes from the man who read her electric meter every month.

If this was friendship, they were off to one heck of a start.

Three

Tripp placed the stethoscope on his young patient's chest. After listening intently to her heartbeat, he moved it around and listened to her lungs. Most of his patients giggled when he did this.

It was all eight-year-old Sierra Rodriguez could do to smile.

"Still not feeling so good?" He spoke in Spanish. The shake of her head was a universal language.

He'd delivered some good news to her parents this morning. The blood tests had ruled out leukemia. The bad news was, she was still running a fever and her belly still hurt. Though Sierra wanted to go home, she needed more tests. She wanted to go home. Migrant workers, her parents didn't have health insurance, money in their pockets or even a permanent home. None of that mattered to Sierra. Home was wherever her family was.

There were hundreds of families just like them in this

part of the country. They were exactly the kind of people Tripp had set up his pilot clinic, located on the outskirts of Ukiah, to help.

The clinic *was* helping, but there was so much more that needed to be done. Medicine cost money. There was no way around it. He could have used a windfall. If he was ever going to expand his pilot program and fund more clinics for the poor in other towns all across California, he needed donations, backers. He needed prestige and contacts, and one way to acquire both was to land and hold that position down in Santa Rosa for a few years, at the very least.

He needed to reconsider Amber's offer. Damn. He had as much trouble swallowing his pride as Sierra had swallowing medicine.

Replacing Sierra's chart, he studied the little girl. Her eyes fluttered closed. She was still very sick. Mentally, he was deciding on the next round of tests. He left the room, deep in thought, his footsteps as heavy as his guilty conscience.

He cringed. He *was* feeling guilty, and he hated it. Amber Colton had said it was a great motivator. Maybe it was true for some people, but it hadn't been guilt over lying to Joe and Meredith Colton all those years ago that had made him strive to be truthful and to do his best. It had been Joe and Meredith, themselves. It was their generosity, their goodness, and the kindness they'd bestowed on him.

Not everyone had ulterior motives. He wondered if it was possible that Amber had offered to act as his fiancée out of the goodness of her heart. Was her offer an act of kindness, and not pity as he'd first suspected? He should have tried to discern which it was. Instead, he'd refused her help, point-blank. And he'd insulted her in the process. He'd seen the hurt in those big green eyes. She'd driven all the way over here to return his watch yesterday, and he hadn't even said thank you.

He wished the hell he would stop thinking about what he should have done or said to her. He wished he could stop thinking about her, period. She'd found her way into his dreams last night, too. He'd awakened in the throes of a strong passion. Not a good way to start a day that promised to be long and frustrating.

He entered his next patient's room. Cisco Villereal grinned at Tripp. The boy was going home today, less his tonsils. Cisco wouldn't miss the infected little bands of tissue, but Tripp was going to miss the six-year-old who, with his family, was heading for the next field and the next harvest.

Kids like Cisco and Sierra made all the grueling days, the long hours, double shifts and hard work worthwhile. Tripp knew doctors who complained that pharmaceutical companies governed modern medicine. It was true that doctors had to shuffle through a boatload of paperwork, but the bottom line remained the same. It was the patient that mattered.

Tripp treated the patient. In the process, he helped the entire family. Often, he could tell how sick the child was by how great the fear in the parent's eyes. Those parents didn't care about hospital politics or red tape or malpractice insurance. If the child was sick enough, they didn't even care about money. They wanted their child well.

It was what Tripp wanted, too. He'd made it his life's work. Not bad for a kid who'd dropped out of school when he was fourteen. He'd dropped out of life before that. Back then, he'd never imagined that someone like him could be anything other than a tough, smart-mouthed street kid whose mother was dead and whose father wasn't around. Kids like him didn't grow up to be doctors. A lot of them didn't grow up at all.

Tripp had been heading down a short road that led nowhere. And hadn't cared. All that began to change the day he was sent to the Hopechest Ranch. From there, it had only been a stone's throw to Joe and Meredith Colton. That stone's throw had changed the entire course of his life.

He'd never set foot inside a hospital until that summer when he was fifteen and Meredith Colton had taken him to the emergency room. He'd busted three bones when his fist had connected with Peter Bradenton's arrogant, better-than-thou face. Fascinated by the buzz and bustle of the hospital emergency room, Tripp had no longer felt any pain. When it was over, his fear that Joe and Meredith would send him away had returned. Not that he'd admitted that, but somehow, Meredith had known. She'd been different back then, kind to her soul, and filled with so much goodness a person ached to make her proud.

Pride was something he'd understood. Pride was all he'd had.

Meredith told him she expected him to apologize to Peter. It hadn't been easy, but for her, Tripp had done it. When he'd finished apologizing, he'd warned Peter what would happen if he were ever unkind to any of the Coltons again.

And then, yesterday, Tripp had been unkind to Amber.

She'd offered to help him. And what had he done? He'd let his pride get in the way of what he needed. If that wasn't bad enough, he'd insulted her.

And he wasn't sure how to fix it.

At the very least, he owed her an apology. He'd picked

up the phone to call her three times last night, only to replace it without completing the call.

An apology like this should be made in person, but he didn't even know where she lived. Once he found out, he planned to drive to her place when his shift was over. He dreaded the confrontation, yet he didn't mind the prospect of seeing Amber again. That bothered him. He liked to think he was immune to curvy, blond and pampered women. The fact that he wasn't was unsettling as hell.

"Good morning, Doctor."

He nodded a greeting at the petite nurse who had spoken. A dozen people were milling about out in the corridor. His eyes homed in on the woman he couldn't get out of his mind.

He stopped so abruptly someone from X-ray ran into him from behind. "Excuse me, doctor," the technician murmured.

"My fault," Tripp said.

He followed Amber around the corner, keeping her in his line of vision as she wove around patients and staff in her path. Tripp believed a man could tell a lot about a woman by the way she walked. Amber Colton had the walk of a woman accustomed to getting a second look. She wasn't oblivious to it, but she didn't seem affected by it, either.

She was wearing another pantsuit, this one white. The top was sleeveless and cinched in at the waist. Her pants were loose in the legs and just snug enough at the hips to lead a man's imagination into dangerous territory. His blood heated, and he scowled.

She was nothing like the kind of woman he needed to look for. She spelled trouble. There was no way around it. But he owed her an apology, and by God, she was going to have one.

"Amber, wait!" It came out as little more than a croak; it was no wonder she didn't hear him.

He lengthened his stride and increased his pace. This time, he kept his eyes trained on something other than the sway of her hips. He focused on the square leather bag hanging from her left shoulder. It swung with every step she took. Every now and then, it moved enough to give him a glimpse of a stuffed dog that was tucked beneath her arm.

She passed the elevator and had almost reached the stairway when he tried again. "Amber, wait!"

This time his voice reached her. She looked over her shoulder and stopped suddenly. He noticed she didn't smile.

"You're not an easy woman to catch up to. Where are you going in such a hurry?"

She glanced at the plush, stuffed brown puppy beneath her arm. "I want to get this up to P.J.'s room. I'm already late for an appointment with the head of charity affairs." She didn't add, "So if you have something to say, say it." She didn't have to. The lift of her eyebrows was a prod if he'd ever seen one.

Tripp wasn't accustomed to being prodded.

"What is it? What are you thinking?" she asked.

He wondered if women had any idea how much men squirmed when asked that question. He blurted the first thing that came to mind. "That you're a bossy woman."

She flushed. And he gave himself a mental shake. He'd angered her again. Or perhaps she was still angry from the day before.

With a lift of her chin, she met his gaze straight on.

"You don't like the way I look, the way I act, the way I talk. What is your problem, Tripp?"

He held up one hand. "I don't think bossiness is necessarily a bad trait. I didn't mean it as an insult."

"You could have fooled me."

She was no shrinking violet, that was for sure. Tripp admired her for it. If she'd been afraid of her own shadow, she never would have had the courage to stand up to her father on his behalf all those years ago. "I didn't stop you to take another cheap shot at you. I stopped you to apologize. For yesterday. And in answer to your earlier question, if I have a problem with you, it's not your fault."

Amber stared up at Tripp. His shirt and tie were black, his skin a shade of brown that didn't need sunscreen. He was clean-shaven this morning and handsome beyond belief. And it ticked her off that she'd noticed. He'd just admitted that his earlier jabs had been cheap shots. In the same breath, he'd admitted that he did, indeed, have a problem with her.

"Whose fault is it then, Tripp? This problem you have with me." Her breath caught in her throat, making her voice sound breathless to her own ears. That ticked her off, too.

"I'm sorry about insulting you yesterday. You didn't ask to be born into a wealthy family any more than I asked to be born into a screwed-up one. It's just that you rich people have no idea how intimidating you are to the rest of us."

He called that an apology? "I...you..." Amber was never at a loss for words, yet here she was, stammering for the second time in a matter of days.

She didn't try to speak again until she'd made certain

she'd put one entire thought in order. "Rich families can be just as dysfunctional as poor ones."

They were arguing about whose family was more dysfunctional? The conversation had sunk to a new low.

He shrugged in a noncommittal, infuriating manner.

"I intimidate you?" she asked.

He released the clasp on his watch, fiddled with it, tightened it again. "Forget it, okay?"

Perhaps she should have let it go, as he'd asked, but that wasn't her style. Yesterday, when she'd seen him again out in the garden at Hacienda de Alegria, she'd felt a connection to him. Ever since her mother had changed and her father had grown distant and her family had basically fallen apart, she'd feared that nobody would ever love her for herself again. Looking at the lines around Tripp's eyes and the furrow between his brows today, she believed it was possible that she'd been wrong. She felt on the brink of understanding something important about him.

Forget it? Now why on earth would she do that? "How do I intimidate you?"

Releasing most of his breath in one noisy stream, he said, "You're brilliant, you're witty, you're rich. You received your MBA from Radcliffe."

"And you're a doctor, for heaven's sake."

Luckily, the corridor was empty, so no one heard him raise his voice as he said, "I'm a struggling, part-Latino, mostly broke doctor who had to work my butt off to make it through med school."

"I distinctly recall my father saying that you graduated at the top of your class."

"The top of my class would have been the bottom of yours."

"I highly doubt that."

He made no reply. So she tried another tactic. "I intimidate you. That's the problem," she said, persisting. "That's what's keeping us from being friends. Let's see. How could we fix it?"

"I don't think we—"

"When I was in grade school and had to give a speech, I used to imagine my classmates in their underwear. Maybe you should try it."

His eyes darkened, his lids lowering slightly.

She ducked her head, pulled a face, and smiled. "On second thought, that's probably not a good idea."

It occurred to Tripp that he was staring. He couldn't help it. The warmth in Amber's smile got to him. He couldn't help that, either. He ran a hand over his hair, skimming the rubber band that secured the stubby ponytail at the back of his neck. He'd kept his ponytail to remind him of where he'd been, and where he was going.

"Coop read me the riot act when he discovered I'd turned down your offer. But you're right. This isn't a good idea. None of it." Not what was in his imagination, not what was coursing through his body. "If I need a woman, it's one who shares my background, my heritage. And I don't need anybody's pity."

Her face fell, a bleak expression settling where her humor had been. She took a backward step. An instant later her chin came up, and her voice rose. "Pity? That's what you think this is about?"

"Aw, hell." He'd done it again.

She handed him the stuffed dog. "I'm late for my meeting. I would appreciate it if you would see that P.J. gets this."

For a long moment, she stared at him without blinking, a burning, faraway look in her eyes. Slowly, she turned, her heels clicking as she walked away from him across the polished, spotless floor.

She paused in the doorway, her back to him, her shoulders rising and falling with her effort to draw a deep, calming breath. "I never felt sorry for you, Tripp." She turned and faced him. "Until now."

She left him standing in the middle of the corridor, his heart beating a heavy rhythm, the ears of the stuffed dog clutched tightly in his fist, sourness in the pit of his stomach, and egg on his face.

Amber ignored her doorbell on her Fort Bragg home the first time it rang. Not five seconds later it rang again, followed immediately by a loud knock that rattled the house. She unfolded her arms and legs and rose from the floor. Hurrying, she raised up on tiptoe to peer through the peephole.

A sound of surprise rose from the back of her throat before she could stop it. Fifteen minutes of meditation, wasted.

She dropped back down to the heels of her feet. Bristling, she reached for the doorknob, but froze in indecision. Her ego was still smarting from her last confrontation with the stubborn, belligerent Dr. Tripp Calhoun.

"Come on, Amber. Open up."

She considered ignoring him. In the end, her curiosity got the better of her. "Give me one good reason why I should."

The moment of silence stretched. Prepared to wait as long as necessary, she shifted her weight to one foot and folded her arms.

"Please?"

He gave her that one word in a voice soft and warm enough to slip into. Her hand flew up to cover her mouth,

gliding slowly down her neck, coming to rest over the
rapid thud of her heart. She took a fortifying breath,
turned the lock and opened the door.

Facing him squarely, she simply looked at him. He was
wearing faded jeans and a black T-shirt that had seen
better days but fit him to perfection. His face was made
up of interesting planes and hard angles. His teeth were
white, his lashes long, his chin firm, his cheekbones
prominent. His nose was narrow and had probably been
considered regal-looking before it had been broken years
ago. He was an arrestingly good-looking man, with just
enough imperfections to ensure that his wasn't a pretty
face. She had artist friends, like Claire, who would love
the chance to paint him. He was that handsome. Amber
knew a lot of handsome men. None of them made her so
angry with seemingly so little effort.

"Please isn't a reason, Calhoun."

His chiseled features cracked slightly, giving her a
glimpse of a self-deprecating half smile. "I'm afraid it's
all I've got."

Her traitorous heart skipped a beat, darn it all. He was
wrong. He had so much more. But who was she to argue?
"What are you doing here?"

"I came to say I'm sorry."

She clasped her hands together and stared at them.
"Your last apology had a lot in common with an insult."

His silence drew her gaze. Studying his lean, olive-
skinned face, her heart lurched. He seemed to be having
difficulty swallowing, too, his lips thinning into a straight
line. "I'm sorry about that, too."

She believed him, which either made her foolish or
desperate. She bristled. Oh, no it didn't.

Squaring her shoulders, she said, "Apology accepted.
Now, if you'll excuse—"

"P.J. loved the stuffed animal."

"He did? I mean, I'm glad."

He held her immobile with his eyes. "And I was thinking that it might be good for him to meet someone like you."

"Someone like me?" She was breathless again. Had she no backbone whatsoever?

"Someone with a strong will, a drive to succeed, a sense of humor and a forgiving spirit."

Evidently not.

She nearly melted into a heap at his feet. Entirely too caught up in her own emotions, she had to remind herself that she was no longer a whimsical girl of nine, or even nineteen. She was a woman, strong and independent.

He looked at her for a long time. Next, he looked beyond her into her foyer where a candle burned and a tabletop fountain gurgled.

"I would be honored if you would invite me in."

The word *honored* was nearly her undoing. It was so old-fashioned, it left her wondering if chivalry was really dead, after all. Thinking "once burned," she took control of her wayward thoughts and said, "You've apologized and I've accepted. What else is there to say?"

She could tell this wasn't easy for him. Groveling never was. She might have let him off the hook, but then she remembered his little quip comparing her to a spoiled cat. And he'd called her bossy.

It wouldn't hurt to let him squirm.

"I've changed my mind, Amber."

"Oh? About what, pray tell?"

"About your offer."

As it often did this time of day, a heavy fog had rolled in, producing a perfect excuse for her shiver. "And what offer was that?'' She didn't know what to blame for the way her voice had dropped in volume.

''Your offer to act as my fiancée at a dinner party this weekend. That is, if the offer still stands.'' He glanced over his shoulder at the sound of voices from a middle-aged couple walking their Great Dane. ''May I come in?''

So, he'd changed his mind about that. She waved at her neighbors, then looked up at Tripp again. She wondered if he'd changed his mind about her, as well. But one thing at a time. She stepped aside, and opened the door all the way.

Tripp walked past Amber. Hesitating in a spacious foyer, he tried to affect an ease he didn't feel. He hadn't been at all certain she would accept his apology. He sure as hell didn't assume that her offer was still good.

''Why don't we sit down?''

Why? Because sitting down meant he had to try even harder to appear relaxed. ''After you.''

He followed her into a small living room dominated by overstuffed furniture and framed artwork done almost entirely in pastels. A dozen candles burned on a low table. A small fountain gurgled nearby. ''Did I interrupt something?''

She shrugged. ''I was meditating.''

At least that explained her appearance. Her hair was in a loose knot on top of her head, flyaway, golden-blond tendrils cascading around her ears and neck. Other than the plain silver ring on her second toe, her feet were bare. Her baggy knit shorts hung below her waist, the front dipping lower than the back. Her top was a sleeveless tank made out of a stretchy fabric that clung to her breasts and bared her midriff. It wasn't as revealing as the bikini she'd been wearing yesterday. It had no business being even more stimulating.

"Smell that?" she said.

For lack of a better plan, he inhaled.

And she said, "It's a blend of lavender, chamomile and rose essential oils. It's called aromatherapy and is supposed to be soothing."

"Did it work?"

"I was getting there. Perhaps you should try it."

He took a quick, sharp breath. So much for trying to appear unaffected.

He could tell she was trying not to smile as she gestured toward an overstuffed, ruffled sofa, indicating that he could take a seat. "Or would you rather stand?"

It was as if she knew him. He shrugged. They both remained standing.

She meandered to the other side of the room. "So you've reconsidered my offer to act as your fiancée at that dinner party."

"Yes."

"I thought you said lies are like dogs."

"They are."

"But?"

"Coop claims playacting and lying are two entirely different things."

"I see. You said Coop read you the riot act because you turned my offer down. Is that why you reconsidered? Because Coop made you see reason?"

"Coop has nothing to do with this. I thought about what you said. About pitying me."

"I shouldn't have said that. It was my temper talking. I'm sorry."

"I had it coming. But I don't want your pity."

"What do you want?"

She must have walked closer when he wasn't looking, because he could see her eyes, round in the dimly lit room, the pupils so large only a narrow circle of green surrounded them. Like pools of appeal, they invited him in. He was in the process of taking his second step when it occurred to him that she wasn't the one who had moved closer.

He needed to loosen his tie. And he wasn't wearing a tie. He settled for clearing his throat. "It isn't about what I want. It's about what I need."

"What do you need, Tripp?"

His gaze strayed to her mouth, his throat convulsing on a swallow. He had to clear it again in order to say, "I need that position in Santa Rosa."

"Why?"

"Santa Rosa is a city of more than a hundred thousand people. It's a wealthy area; the practice is a private one with new, modern, state-of-the-art equipment. The facility is only a thirty-minute drive from San Francisco and caters to the wealthy. My salary would more than triple. I need the money and the prestige."

She looked him in the eye and said, "You don't strike me as the type who cares about prestige."

He told himself he had no business feeling complimented. "It isn't for me. It's for a clinic I've set up to aid the poor. Right now, it's operating on a shoestring. I want to expand it in this area. Eventually I plan to open a dozen more up and down the California coast. It's going to take donations, and backers with deep pockets."

"Why didn't you say so?" She asked a hundred intelligent questions. And he, a man who preferred yes and no answers, poured out the story of the clinic's meager beginnings, and his hopes and plans for its future. Sometime during the conversation, he'd taken a seat on her comfortable sofa and she'd sat in the matching chair, her bare feet tucked underneath her.

Maybe there was something to that aromatherapy after all.

The sky outside her windows went from milky white to gray to pitch black. The candles burned low; she didn't turn on a light. Sometimes, their conversation flickered like that candlelight, illuminating other topics, her brothers and sisters and a few of the foster kids he'd known while staying with her family. She spoke lovingly of her father, but never mentioned her mother. She seemed concerned about her oldest brother, Rand, and was worried because she hadn't heard from her younger, adopted sister, Emily. It occurred to him that he didn't know Amber well. He'd lost touch with most of the Coltons. Other than staying in contact with Joe, Tripp had been too busy clawing his way through med school to maintain strong ties with the huge, extended Colton clan. He hadn't even known Emily had left town and hadn't contacted anybody. He hadn't known that Amber lived in Fort Bragg, either. Inez had been only too happy to supply him with that information when he'd shown up at the ranch in Prosperino earlier. Funny, he'd expected Amber to live in a grand house like her father's, but her home was quite modest.

She didn't seem to want to talk about herself, though. Every time it happened, she steered the conversation back to his pilot clinic or the position he was after in Santa Rosa.

"How many times have you met with the doctors at this exclusive practice?"

"Two."

"How many times has your rival met with the same people?"

"I don't know."

She procured a notebook out of nowhere, and began jotting things down. She wanted to know about the dinner, and who would be attending. She was professional, exuberant, warm and smart. God yes, she was smart. He was in awe.

The wind rattled a window. Although he didn't feel a draft, the candles flickered.

Their gazes met, held. The images from his dreams the previous night shimmered through his mind. His breathing deepened, his gaze skimming over her body.

"What are you doing tomorrow?" she asked.

"Working." He cleared his throat. At least she hadn't asked him what he was thinking. It was a good thing, because he would have been even more hard pressed to come up with a good answer.

"What time could you be finished?"

"Four or five."

"Think you could come back to Fort Bragg around five?"

"You want me to come back?"

She looked at him with a lift of her eyebrows that seemed to say, "Isn't that what I just said?" But she only nodded.

After a moment, he did, too.

She wrote something in her notebook, tore the page out and tucked it into his hand. "Meet me at this address, say, at five o'clock. We'll begin the tweaking then."

Tweaking?

He'd be damned if he would let his imagination go there. He rose quickly to his feet.

Despite his best efforts, he got a mental picture and warmed ten degrees. She was circling him. It gave him a moment to get his body under control.

"What do you mean, tweaking?"

"At this point," she said from a place directly behind him, "appearance is everything. There's a wonderful old-world men's clothing store right here in Fort Bragg."

He peered at the address on the sheet of paper in his hand. "A men's clothing store? You want me to buy a new suit? That's what you meant?"

"Unless you already own a dynamite one. What did you think I meant?"

Never mind what he'd thought. "Dr. Perkins has already seen me like this."

She looked him over. "There's certainly nothing wrong with the way you are. Not from a female's perspective. This Dr. Perkins doesn't happen to be a woman, does she?"

He shook his head.

And she sighed. "Too bad. Oh, well. This weekend, we're going to give the people affiliated with Dr. Perkins's practice a new and improved version of Dr. Tripp Calhoun, the finest pediatrician in sunny California."

She ushered him to the door. Although he didn't remember doing it, he must have opened it, because he walked through.

"Tripp?"

He turned on the top step. "Yes?"

"I'm glad we're going to be friends again." Before he could answer, she reached up on tiptoe and brushed her lips across his. "Good night."

The door closed. He didn't recall saying goodbye, either, but he must have. At least he hoped he had.

He wet his lips, and tasted the strawberry flavor of her lip gloss. He wiped it off with the back of his hand, and stood statue-still, desire uncurling deep inside him.

Whoa. He appreciated Amber's offer to help, and he

would tell her so. After that, he was going to have to lay out a few ground rules. He needed this position, and the credibility it would bring. Okay, maybe he even needed a new suit. If she thought he would bleach his hair and wear blue contacts, she was mistaken. If he got that position, it would be because of who he was, the man inside, not the trappings.

They were going to pretend to be engaged. He didn't like the idea of lying, even if it was under the guise of pretending. But he didn't see any other way.

He and Amber were already becoming friends. That part was real. He would hold it there. There would be no real passion between them.

He would tell her as soon as he saw her tomorrow. He started for his nondescript, dependable car and got in. Now, he thought, trying to find a comfortable position in jeans that were suddenly a good size too small, if only somebody would break it to his body.

Four

"Oh, my, I do believe we've found the one!"

Tripp tried not to wince, honest to God he did, but if André's voice got any shriller, the trifold mirror was going to shatter.

"It has style. It says class with a capital C, and it fits you to perfection. Perfection, I say!" André's eyebrows were chestnut-colored slashes above startling brown eyes that didn't come close to matching the yellow streaks in his short-cropped hair. "Don't you agree, Amber?"

Tripp met Amber's gaze in the mirror. She smiled demurely. "This jacket looks good, too, André."

The double entendre was lost on André. "Good? It looks glorious. What do you think, Doctor?"

Tripp thought he would have more fun having a kidney transplant. "It's black," he said. Every suit jacket he'd tried on had been black.

André looked to Amber for emotional support. She

said, "Black is a formal, classic color that never goes out
of style. You can wear it to weddings and funerals, fine
restaurants, important galas and everything in between.
Montgomery Perkins was born with a silver spoon in his
mouth. He and his family moved to California from the
East Coast twenty-five years ago. His bloodline can be
traced back to the Mayflower and beyond. He's the type
of man who would own a closet full of black suits, and
expect others to, as well."

Tripp stared at her. "How do you know that?"

She shrugged, then examined her fingernails. "I
checked him out. Apparently he's a very traditional and
wealthy physician, one who wouldn't appreciate a candidate showing up wearing a clown nose or tweed."

André fanned himself at her mention of tweed. "Have
we found the perfect one, or shall we continue?"

Tripp studied his own reflection. The jacket looked
okay. It fit okay. It felt okay. He shrugged. "How
much?"

André named an obscene amount. This time Tripp
didn't even attempt to hide his wince. He'd tried on a
dozen jackets, and every one of them cost more than he
paid for an entire month's rent. There were dozens more,
hell, a hundred more in the store. A kidney transplant
was looking better all the time.

He eyed his reflection once more. "Fine," he said
without inflection. "I'll take it."

André beamed. "Now for the pants, shirt and tie. I
was thinking a shirt in gray, perhaps, just the right shade,
of course, and a tie in—" Just then, the phone rang.
André threw up his hands. "That'll be Jules wondering
what's keeping me. Excuse me while I take the call. I'll
be right back with those pants and other items." He
flounced away.

"I can hardly wait," Tripp said under his breath.

"You know, Tripp," Amber said quietly, "you could learn something from watching André."

Tripp glanced to the front of the store where the other man was reaching for a phone. "What could I learn?"

"How to schmooze."

He shuddered inwardly at the thought.

"And it wouldn't hurt to smile."

"I smile."

"When?"

He gave her a blank stare and a phony smile.

She shook her head. "That doesn't count. When was the last time you smiled and meant it?"

He drew a real blank and gave a genuine scowl.

She slanted him a victorious look. "I have several more suggestions and hints to help you gain your new position. For now, it might be better if we changed the subject. André is wonderful, isn't he?"

"Glorious."

Amber looked at him with a lift of her eyebrows he found intriguing as hell. "Could you at least try to curtail your enthusiasm?" When he didn't reply, she said, "Now what's wrong?"

Wrong? What could possibly be wrong? Aside from the fact that he didn't have the time for this, or the patience, let alone the money. But that wasn't her fault.

He shrugged out of the jacket, then turned in a half circle, searching for a place to unload it. "I was just calculating how many children Miguel Rodriguez could feed for what I'm going to pay for just one of these dark suits."

She took the coat from him and folded it carefully over her arm. "For the cost of one suit, you'll be helping hundreds of families like Miguel's."

Tripp didn't quite know what to say to that. She had a point. She also had an amazing body and a face to match. He chastised himself for noticing. Unlike department stores, this exclusive, European-style men's clothing store was illuminated by strategically placed wall fixtures, the bulbs glimmering through frosted glass sconces. It threaded Amber's hair with spun gold and gave her skin a soft-as-twilight glow. Tripp had never believed clothes made the man. Or the woman, either, for that matter. It was a good thing, because his discount store cotton shirt and navy chinos were in stark contrast to her designer slacks and silk blouse. Her shoes were Haan loafers. Tripp didn't know what the hell that meant, but evidently they must have been expensive, because André had beamed his approval during their discussion of head-to-toe image.

"You're scowling again, Calhoun."

"Do you always have to have the last word?" he asked.

She surveyed him kindly. "Only when I'm right."

"Have you ever been wrong?"

"Not that I recall."

She moved with an easy grace that caused the light to catch in the elegant folds in her silk blouse. The playful glint in her eyes had nothing to do with artificial lighting.

"At least it hasn't gone to your head."

The tart grinned. "You have your gifts, I have mine. It was awfully good of André to keep the store open for you."

"I told you. An emergency held me up at the hospital in Ukiah. I raced the wind to get here as fast as I could."

"No easy feat over the hairpin curves and snaking trail they call State Road 20."

Tripp shrugged, and thought out loud. "I enjoy that

kind of driving. It allows a man to think, but not too hard.''

"Is that what men like? To think, but not too hard?"

He stared at her, trying to decide if she was flirting with him, baiting him or just having fun. Witty and articulate, she picked up on subtle nuances and gave as good as she got. He couldn't remember the last time he'd had so much trouble matching wits with another adult. Kids sometimes surprised him, but few women did. Something strange was going on here. Why, he was starting to almost enjoy himself. He reeled the thought back in. This was business, a means to an end. The fact that he and Amber had known each other a long time ago complicated it slightly, but only slightly, and definitely only temporarily.

No matter what he'd insinuated, he'd spent the hourlong drive navigating the hilly road thinking about her. So far, he hadn't had a chance to lay out any of those ground rules he'd considered last night. First, he had something even more important to do. Easing a step closer, he said, "Thank you."

Her face came up, her eyes wide, her lips parting. She was so obviously startled, he did something completely uncustomary. He grinned.

Her gaze flicked over him, and her eyes seemed to have gotten stuck on his mouth. He couldn't help goading her. "You told me to smile."

"Yes," Amber said quietly. "I did."

Amber hadn't intended her voice to dip so low or sound so sultry, but darn it all, she hadn't expected his voice to work over her in soft waves, either. It weakened her knees. This, she told herself, was what she got for being bossy. A warm, delicious shiver started in that sensitive little spot between her shoulder blades. It moved downward and outward, all the way to her fingers and toes. She was completely taken with this man. She sighed, because her infatuation was about as handy as pockets on a space suit.

She recalled the mild panic she'd experienced earlier when Tripp had been five minutes late, ten, fifteen. Her panic had turned into dread long before an hour had been up. She didn't understand what was happening to her. Tripp Calhoun was an enigma, and a challenge. And more.

She liked him. Go figure. More important, she wanted him to like her. Which was ridiculous, not to mention immature. Why should she care if he liked her?

She cared.

He made her care. By not caring that she cared.

She wanted to throw her hands in the air the way André had. It was ridiculous. And yet it wasn't. Every time she came near Tripp everything felt exciting and brand-new. Her breathing became shallow, her heart sped up and her thoughts turned as hazy as a long-forgotten dream.

He wasn't an easygoing man. But he was sincere about it. He sincerely cared about people. It was there in the low rumble of his voice when he'd spoken to little P.J. a few days ago, and when he'd said thank you a moment ago. That reminded her—

"For what?" she asked.

He looked at her long and hard for a moment before saying, "I beg your pardon?"

"You thanked me. What was that for?"

"For not giving me the third degree when I was an hour late. For nodding agreeably when André exclaimed that each suit coat looked better than the last, when we both know damn well they all looked the same. For researching Montgomery Perkins and his medical practice. You're very thorough.''

See, she told herself, he was sincere. Oh, at times he was cross and sullen, too. But she could see past that. She was almost afraid to hope that before her stood a man who might, just might, want to look beyond her exterior and try to discover who she really was on the inside, where it truly mattered.

Just in case she was imagining things, she moved in closer, studying him.

''What are you doing?'' Tripp breathed deeply, catching a whiff of exotic perfume that went straight to his head. Or maybe Amber's smile had done that.

''Who are you?'' she asked. ''And what have you done with Tripp Calhoun?''

Something stirred inside Tripp, something restless and unwelcome, and completely irreverent. Damn, it felt good. He needed to get to those ground rules, and soon. ''That wasn't very original. I read that it takes twelve acts of kindness to make up for one negative one, and since I still have eleven positives to bestow, I'll let it go this time.''

Her smile grew. ''You're being nice because you want to make up for yesterday?''

''The thought crossed my mind.''

Again with that smile.

He tried to figure out what it was about her that drew him. Nothing about the conversation should have been lust-arousing, and yet awareness simmered between them. He shrugged a shoulder, easing closer as if it were the most natural thing in the world. She looked at him, her eyes bright, her face upturned, her lips parted slightly. He was tempted to kiss her, here and now. The idea burned in his mind, heating his blood another degree with every inch he lowered his face toward hers.

"That Jules!" A shrill voice sounded behind them.

Tripp and Amber jerked apart, then pretended interest in opposite directions as casually as they could manage.

"Always wanting to know when I'll be home. Now for those pants!" André was back, talking a mile a minute. "These are to die for. And this tie, hmm-humm."

Tripp cleared his throat and tried to clear the roaring din from his mind and his ears. He glanced at Amber, only to drag his gaze away when André brought a measuring tape from his pocket and glided down to one knee.

"What are you doing?"

André swatted Tripp's hand aside. "I need to measure your inseam."

For a moment, Tripp froze.

"That's it. Hold nice and still."

Nice and still, hell. Tripp backed up so fast André nearly fell over. He caught himself at the last minute with one hand pressed to the floor.

The bell over the front door jangled, signaling the arrival of another customer despite the closed sign in the window. André cast Tripp a questioning look before rushing off with a flourish toward the front of the store.

"What did you do that for?" Amber asked.

Tripp gritted his teeth. "I stopped growing years ago. I don't need my inseam measured." He noticed Amber's grim expression. He didn't understand it, but at that point, he had more important things to do than try to figure it out.

"Especially not by a man who lives with an artist named Jules, is that it?" she asked.

She pried the measuring tape from his fisted hand

while his mind was still blank. Long before he figured out what the hell she was talking about, she continued.

"For your information, Jules is a nickname."

"So?"

"Short for Juliann. With two n's."

"You're saying Jules is a woman?"

Her eyes darkened with an emotion he couldn't identify. "That's what you get for stereotyping."

That was when it occurred to Tripp that she'd gone down to her knees exactly as André had. "What are you doing?"

"Somebody has to measure your inseam."

His hand shot out, covering hers an inch away from its targeted area. "I wasn't stereotyping, dammit. And I'm not having you measure my inseam, either." Not in the state he was in.

"You're not?" And then, in a softer voice, "You weren't?"

She was still on her knees, and she was looking straight ahead. She averted her eyes the way a highbred lady should. The smile that stole across her face, however, wasn't the smile of a genteel woman of high social standing. It was playful and bratty, and made Tripp even more uncomfortable.

"Of course you weren't." She rose blithely to her feet.

She seemed buoyant and happy suddenly. And beautiful. He clamped his mouth shut. And sensual.

A lot of women were sensual. Hell, most of them were. He had damn good reasons for fighting the attraction crackling between him and this particular one. And as soon as the blood returned to his brain, he'd be able to recall every one of them.

"Relax, Tripp."

Easy for her to say. "What makes you think I'm not relaxed?"

She touched three fingers to his watch, which happened to be twirling around his finger instead of resting on his wrist where it belonged. He thought it was very big of her to refrain from expounding upon the obvious. He probably should have told her he appreciated her restraint. He had eleven more positive gestures to make, after all.

She handed him the measuring tape. "Here," she said, far too sweetly for his peace of mind. "Why don't you do the honors?"

He tossed the tape to a nearby chair. "Just help me find a pair of dress pants in my size, all right?"

She smiled, slow and dreamy. "Whatever you say, Doctor. Whatever you say."

She was laughing on the inside. He knew it, and he understood it. What he didn't understand was why he felt no anger.

He thought about picking a fight just to get back on track, but she'd already started for a rack in the middle of the store. And Tripp didn't have much choice but to follow her.

Tripp unlocked his car door and moved to toss the new suit and all its accessories inside. Amber caught his hand before he'd released the zippered, plastic bag. With utmost care, she squeezed past him and hung the suit from the little hook over the back door.

Watching the way she contorted and wiggled her body in order to arrange the suit in a way so as not to wrinkle it reminded him that his credit card wasn't the only thing overheated. Not that he needed reminding.

"What do you want to do now?" she asked, backing up.

He forced his eyes away from the part of her heading right for him. "I have to get back to Ukiah."

"So soon?" She closed his car door with one hand, then brushed imaginary wrinkles from her slacks. Every movement was naturally feminine, and far too luxuriant for a man in Tripp's frame of mind. Especially since he wasn't supposed to be looking at her in the first place.

He took a deep breath.

"Doesn't that smell lovely?" she asked conversationally. "When the breeze is right, like it is tonight, the air is filled with the scent of hundreds of flowers and shrubs growing in the botanical gardens just south of Fort Bragg."

Tripp was familiar with several of the small towns in the north-central portion of California, but not many along the coast. He'd lived in L.A. until he was fifteen. Back then, his world had consisted of apartments, housing projects, deserted buildings and back alleys in his neighborhood. He'd spent seven years at the University of California in San Francisco. This was his first visit to Fort Bragg. He'd heard of the Skunk Railroad, named for the noxious fumes the engine had pumped out back when the railway had been used to cart lumber across the coastal mountains between Fort Bragg and Willitis. He needed to be heading back that way, himself.

"Tripp?"

"Hmm?"

"Are you hungry or aren't you?"

Obviously, she'd been talking. He really needed to pay attention. He gave her a gesture she interpreted as a nod.

"Shall we grab a bite to eat?"

"Here?"

"Did you have someplace else in mind?"

The shake of his head served a dual purpose. It answered her question and attempted to clear his mind of what was really in it. "To tell you the truth, I'm going to be eating peanut butter for a while."

"Oh."

Before they parted, there was something he had to say. "About what almost happened between us in the store..."

"What almost happened between us?"

He felt sideswiped by her smile. "I came damn close to kissing you, and you know it."

"Oh, that."

A warning gong went off in Tripp's head. "Amber," he said.

Air brakes hissed on the street behind them. Laying a hand on her elbow, he drew her with him to the relative safety of the sidewalk. "I appreciate what you're trying to do for me. I'm not poetic enough to word this right, but I want to get something straight between us."

"What's on your mind, Tripp?"

Forget what was on his mind. This had to be said. "We come from different backgrounds, different places. Our paths crossed once, and I'm not sorry they're crossing again. But that's all this is. A crossroads. I'm no expert on women, but the ones I've known place a hell of a lot more importance on a kiss, even on a near-kiss, than men do. I'd hate to see you get hurt, and I'd hate even more to be the one responsible for hurting you."

The evening breeze stirred the awnings over the quaint stores lining the main thoroughfare in Fort Bragg's downtown district. That same breeze tugged a lock of Tripp's dark hair from the rubber band at his nape. Amber fought the urge to reach up with gentle fingertips and tuck it back in. Her gaze met his, and a zing went through her. For an instant, she saw hunger in his eyes, not necessarily for food.

He wanted her. He didn't want to, but he did. Suddenly, it was all-important that she didn't lose the fight before she'd even gotten into the ring. "I'm a big girl. I'm perfectly capable of taking care of myself, but fine, I've been duly warned. You're off the hook. We have a lot of work to do between now and this weekend. My car's parked at the end of the next block. You can walk me to it while I outline my plans. Please don't just stand there. Time's a-wasting."

She spun around and started down the sidewalk, her heart in her throat. She didn't draw an easy breath until Tripp fell into step beside her.

"You always were bossy."

She bit her lip. "I said please."

His brown eyes were fixed straight ahead. "You meant just do it, dammit. Or else."

"Not or else." She smiled. She thought it was very gentlemanly of him not to mention that she hadn't disputed the rest of it. It was as if he understood her—and he liked her anyway. This tall, rugged man who rarely concerned himself with others' impressions of him liked her.

She glanced sideways at him. "You might as well say it."

Tripp had a feeling that somewhere in the dark recesses of her mind, Amber knew exactly what she was doing. He on the other hand, had no idea what she was talking about, and this time, he'd been paying attention. "I might as well say what?"

"Whatever it is that had you scowling at that poor woman we just met."

"What poor woman?" he asked in spite of himself.

"The one who just took one look at you and gave you a five-foot berth. She's probably had a horrible day, had to work late, and is hurrying home to her hungry kids."

"She was hurrying home to her cats."

"How do you know that?"

"She was carrying a bag of cat food. See that woman over there just getting out of her minivan?"

"The thin redhead?"

He nodded. "She's completely frazzled. And that heavyset one crossing the street? She enjoys being a woman. A lot."

Amber stopped so suddenly the people walking behind her nearly ran into her. Tripp went a few steps without her, then stopped, too. "Is that what you men do?" she asked when he'd turned to face her. "You make blind assumptions about women when you watch us?"

"They're not blind assumptions." He lowered his voice in direct response to the pointed looks they were getting. "And I don't know about all men. It isn't something men discuss."

"But you're saying you can tell a lot about a woman by the way she walks."

He nodded as if he thought it was completely unnecessary to reply.

This was the moment of truth, Amber thought, the moment when she discovered how he saw her. It was a risk to her ego, and possibly to her heart. She took a deep breath. Here goes nothing. "What can you tell about me?"

He settled his feet a more comfortable distance apart and folded his arms at his chest. "You're a woman who's accustomed to getting a second look and her own way."

She wanted to ask if that was all he saw, but she didn't.

Instead, she said, "And was this revealed when I was walking toward you or away?"

"Away." He didn't even have to think about it. "Definitely away."

"What about when I'm walking toward you?"

"That's confusing."

"What's confusing about me, Tripp?"

"What isn't? You're gorgeous and you know it. But you're also golden, like sunshine. You have a smart mouth and a serene smile. And your eyes, well, they're like soft grass one minute, cool shade the next. Confusing as hell."

He started walking again. As Amber fell into step beside him, her heart teetered on her breastbone. From there it was an easy slide into her stomach. "And you said you're not poetic."

He didn't appear nearly as pleased about that as she.

She stopped near the front bumper of her shiny red sports car. "Here we are. I'll call you tomorrow."

"Amber, wait. This conversation isn't finished."

She looked over her shoulder at him. "Were you this quarrelsome with your former fiancée?"

He narrowed his eyes and glared at her. Unlike the woman they'd seen moments ago and who right now was driving by in a car bearing a bumper sticker that read, Dogs have owners, cats have staff, Amber wasn't intimidated by Tripp in the least. "What was your fiancée's name again? Olive-Oyl?"

"That'd be *former* fiancée. And her name was Olivia." His voice held no humor.

Amber reached inside her big, square purse. Finding her notebook gave her something do to with her hands and a reason to avert her face so he couldn't see the little roll she gave her eyes. "Olivia what?"

"Babcock."

She turned so fast the pen she'd put to paper made a bold line across the blank page. "Olivia Babcock, daughter of Jamison Babcock, the man who amassed his fortune back when the computer industry was a new frontier and has since turned his attention as well as a huge share of his money to cancer research?"

"You know them?"

Not personally. But she'd heard of them. Olivia Babcock grew up near L.A. She'd been closer to Sophie's age than Amber's, and had been in the society pages since birth. She was glamorous, sophisticated, beautiful. She and Tripp had once been engaged? Amber wondered if he'd loved her. He must have. She wondered if he still did.

"Do you miss her?"

He made no reply.

It was like pulling teeth. "Do you ever see her?"

"I thought I would be seeing her this weekend."

Amber was getting a bad feeling about this.

"But it turns out I was wrong," he said. "She and her new fiancé are having dinner with Dr. and Mrs. Perkins tonight and won't be attending our gathering in Santa Rosa on Saturday. Praise the Lord."

Amber didn't know whether to be as elated as Tripp. "Let me ask you something," she said. "Don't you think it's awfully strange that your ex just happens to be engaged to Derek Spencer? The same Derek Spencer who's the contender for the position you're after?"

Tripp's answer was a sharp nod.

Amber could have spent an hour deciphering the expression deep in his eyes. Releasing a low whistle, she said, "Strange, my eye. That is some coincidence."

"I thought so, too."

"I don't know how to break this to you, Doctor, but if your contender has the Babcock name behind him, you're going to need more than great credentials and a new suit."

"The Colton name carries its own power and prestige, Amber."

A worrisome little pounding started in her temples and worked its way around to her forehead. She was digging herself into a deep hole. She wanted to help Tripp, but she wanted to be more than a trophy on his arm. She wanted to be his… His what? His friend. And perhaps even his lover?

She pushed the question away and concentrated on the matter at hand. "Maybe you'd better tell me a little more about this dinner we'll be attending this weekend."

She leaned a hip against her car door. Tripp's back remained ramrod straight, his feet set firmly apart, his hands on his hips as he said, "Cocktails begin at seven. Dinner is at eight."

"Where?"

"Ever hear of a place called Alessandro's?"

Heard of it? Anyone who was anyone had dined at the world-renowned, five-star French restaurant. "Whose idea was it to meet there?"

"One of the doctors in Perkins's practice owns shares in it."

Oh. She'd missed that. She started jotting things in her notebook again. "Be at my place Thursday at eight."

"For what?"

"For dinner, of course. Better yet, meet me at Hacienda de Alegria. I'm a fair cook at best. I'll see if Inez would mind helping."

"Helping do what?"

"Arrange a place setting and create a scenario similar

to the one we'll encounter this weekend. You'll be scrutinized down to the tiniest detail. And you'll be judged
on more than your new suit, believe me. *Our* table manners will have to be impeccable.''

Tripp's hands slid from his hips to his sides, where he
squeezed them into fists. *Our* table manners, hell. It reminded him of the nurses who breezed into a patient's
room and asked how ''we're'' feeling. Amber meant *he*
was going to be judged on more than a new suit and
table manners, when he should be judged on his medical
knowledge and bedside manner, dammit. What really angered him was Amber's assumption that he didn't know
enough not to slurp his soup.

He'd been so intrigued by her sunny disposition and
so busy being attracted to her that he'd forgotten she was
rich, pampered and the complete opposite of the kind of
woman he needed. Except he did need her, at least for
Saturday night. And that angered him the most.

''Eight o'clock,'' he said, commending himself for his
discipline and quiet reserve. ''I'll see you then.'' He
turned on his heel and walked away without another
word.

Amber was left standing next to her car, watching his
footsteps burn up the sidewalk. He was angry. What
now?

It might have had something to do with her mention
of his former fiancée, his contender, or her. He could
have stuck around long enough for her to find out. But
no, that wasn't his way.

He was honorable and ornery. Impatient one minute,
sincere the next, difficult without a doubt. He had a chip
on his shoulder and a burning glimmer in his eyes. He
liked her, and didn't seem especially thrilled about it. He
could hold his own in a conversation with her, no easy

feat for most people. She didn't understand half of what drove him. He was a lot of man. Her father always said it would take a lot of man to make her happy.

Wouldn't you know, he was exactly the kind of man she could love.

"How long were you and Olivia Babcock engaged?"

"Not long."

Amber stared over the flickering candles, waiting for Tripp to continue. When he did, it was to change the subject.

"It's a good thing the restaurant has a five-star rating. If the lights are this dim Saturday night, we'll need to use the light from those five stars to see what we're eating."

Lucky for him she'd seen his good side, because if she hadn't, she would be sorely tempted to dump a glass of lemon ice water over his arrogant head. She was tempted anyway.

She lowered her salad fork to her salad plate, took her napkin from her lap, pushed her chair out slightly and rose slowly to her feet. From there, it was an easy march to the far wall where she turned up the lighting. "How's that, better?"

He'd arrived at her parents' home right on time. Inez had answered the door while Amber was putting the finishing touches on the place settings in the formal dining room. After arranging the food on the buffet according to course, and covering each dish with polished silver lids, Inez had been only too happy to retreat to the small home she and her husband, Marco, shared on the grounds of Hacienda de Alegria. Amber's father was in Washington D.C. on business, and Meredith was in the theater room with the two youngest, and by far most spoiled

Coltons, Teddy and Joe, Jr. That left Amber and Tripp alone in this wing of the Colton home.

"Well?" Amber had asked, proud of her handiwork. "What do you think?"

Tripp had eyed the ornate centerpiece and fine linen place mats and napkins. "How many plates and forks can one person use?"

Evidently, a good night's sleep hadn't improved his disposition. She'd traipsed to her chair, thinking it was amazing that the man could remain upright with that heavy chip on his shoulder. She took her seat, saying, "I'm perfectly capable of pulling out my own chair, but it will look better if you do it for me on Saturday. For now, let's collaborate on our stories."

"Our stories?"

"Yes. How did we meet? How long have we been seeing each other? That sort of thing."

"Collaborate on our lies, you mean."

She'd stared at him over the tops of the candles. "You're right. Let's stick as close to the truth as possible. We met when we were kids, and then bumped into each other again recently here at my father's house. We'll make certain to drop Dad's name at least three times. And if we're going to be convincing, we're going to have to gaze lovingly into each other's eyes several times. A stretch of the imagination, I know. We're going to have to practice." If her voice had become droll, she couldn't help it. "And one more thing, Tripp."

He paused, his fork in midair, then slowly lowered it to the table. "What?"

She didn't know how to bring this up delicately. "You'll look stunning in your new suit. But if you want to look respectable, you really need to consider cutting your hair."

He didn't have it secured in a rubber band tonight. It was shiny and straight and chin-length. The way he'd tucked it behind his ears made him look as if he'd stepped from another time. He could have been a pirate, or a knight, or a conquistador.

His eyes glimmered like glass across the table. "No."

She did a double take. "What do you mean, no?"

Tripp spread his hands wide on either side of his plate. "It's a little word, one syllable, two letters. Or aren't the rich familiar with the concept?"

"I know what no means. What I don't know is why you're trying to start a fight. You're the one who wants that position. I'm only trying to help."

The way he scratched his chin looked completely out of character. "Contrary to what you think, I have my pride."

"What's that supposed to mean?"

"I won't be judged on appearance alone."

If that wasn't the pot calling the kettle black. Appearance was important, but there was more to people than that. Amber's mother used to say it was what was on the inside that counted. It had been years since her mother had even tried to see inside Amber's heart. Her little sister Emily had, but Emily had left Prosperino months ago.

Amber had hoped that she would find a man who looked past the part of her she showed the world, to the part she kept hidden from all but a select few. She wasn't a fanciful woman, or a particularly romantic one. She knew her strengths and weaknesses. She was a modern-day woman with a fair mind, a smart mouth and an honest soul. And she honestly didn't know what to do about the spiteful, snide man sitting across the table from her right now.

She decided to try one more time. "That new suit will

get your foot in the door. After that, it's up to you to show Perkins what you're made of.''

''Then you're saying actions speak louder than words?''

She nodded. Finally, they were getting somewhere.

He picked up the finger bowl and took a loud slurp.

The room, all at once, was perfectly quiet. He'd made his point. Another time she might have commended him for his aplomb. This wasn't another time. This was now, and right now she'd had it with his attitude.

A small chunk of her crusty bread bounced off his forehead and splashed in his water goblet. Amber didn't know who was more surprised.

Tripp stared at her, as if he couldn't believe what he was seeing. Surely it was the devil that made her tear off a second piece.

''What the hell are you doing?''

''What does it look like I'm doing?'' She dipped the second glob of bread in her finger bowl.

''It looks like you're lowering yourself to my level.''

The soggy bread hit him in the center of his stubborn, spiteful, arrogant chin.

''I'm sick and tired of your snide comments and condescending attitude, Doctor.''

''*My* attitude? I'm not the one who's making sure I don't embarrass them at the dinner table this Saturday.''

''That's what you think I'm doing?''

''I know which fork to use. Olivia made certain of that.''

She rose to her feet, only her fingertips touching the polished surface of the table. ''Did it ever occur to you that maybe I invited you here so we could brush up together?'' She wanted to throttle him. Shaking slightly, she added, ''And because I like you?'' She eyed the homemade bread in her hand. Forget breaking it into small pieces. She flung what was left of her crusty roll at him in a way reminiscent of her tomboy days; her brothers would have been proud.

Both held perfectly still, each assessing the other's anger. She liked him? Tripp thought. He glimpsed a moment's hurt in her green eyes. Hell, she liked him.

He brushed crumbs from his shirt, then fished a soggy morsel from his lap. Next, he pushed his chair back and very casually reached for his linen napkin. After placing it to the right of all his dinner paraphernalia, he found his feet. "I thought you were... I shouldn't have, I know. It's just that—"

She held up one hand. Slowly, painstakingly, she retrieved the pedestal bowl containing the peach-flavored crème brûlée from the sideboard. Tripp's gaze followed her movements. She didn't intend... She wouldn't...

Staring at the heaping spoon in her hand, he said, "We both know it would be completely beneath you to do what you're thinking about doing."

The lumpy goo landed an inch higher than the roll had. Tripp looked down just as the dessert lost its fight with gravity and plopped to the top of his shoe.

"All right, Amber. You've made your point. I misjudged you. You have no idea how sorry I am. I won't let it happen again."

She scooped a dollop onto one finger, then licked the end of it. It was provocative as hell. "You're wrong," she said with saccharine sweetness. "I know just how sorry you are. You're a sorry, snide, prideful man who's been carrying a chip on his shoulder long enough. You think you have the corner market on pride? What do you think of this?"

Think?

He was too busy ducking to think. A second, much larger dollop of crème brûlée missed his ear by a fraction of an inch. He heard it land somewhere behind him.

He stared at her for interminable seconds. He picked up his napkin and dabbed at the dark spot on his shirt. Then, eyes narrowed, he walked to the sideboard and speared a piece of shrimp scampi with his fork.

"What are you doing?" she asked.

He drew the fork back like a slingshot. "As you can see, I'm using the correct fork. And for the record, you started this."

Her eyebrows rose in the semidarkness. He was glad she'd turned the lights up, because he wouldn't have wanted to miss the way her eyes glittered with excitement.

"That," she taunted, "is what Custer shouted to the Indians at Little Big Horn while making his last stand. Shall I refresh your memory as to how that turned out for Custer?"

"Refresh this!" The shrimp scampi arced through the air.

Amber screeched, clamored, and ducked, but not fast enough. The shrimp caught in her hair. She threw down the spoon and scooped up the crème brûlée with her bare hand. "That does it, Calhoun. This means war!"

Five

Tripp moved stealthily around the table, taking his eyes off Amber only long enough to glance at the remaining serving dishes and bowls, and consider his options. Shrimp scampi and crusty bread had sufficed as attention-getters, but they were no competition for the cold, wet goo that had splattered one side of his face moments ago. The bowl of crème brûlée was his best bet, but it was closer to Amber. He continued around the table, hoping to lure her away from it. She beat him to it, whisking it out of his reach.

The woman was cunning and quick. She could have given some of the kids from his old neighborhood a few pointers and a run for their money. The thought bothered the back of his mind. He reminded himself that these weren't the streets of L.A. Amber was safe here. At least, he thought, taking an ominous step closer, she was safe from harm.

He considered his remaining choices. There was a bowl of seafood rice stuffing, coffee and creamer, some green, leafy things she'd called salad and he called weeds, and a little dish of melted butter. He was going to have to make do with the bowl of rice stuffing. With lightning-quick movements reminiscent of his cagey, street-fighting days, he whisked it from the buffet table and into his left hand. Next, he eased around Amber's chair as she eased around his. They moved in the same direction, counterclockwise, keeping the gleaming cherrywood table between them.

The shrimp looked out of place in her hair. She made no move to brush it out, nor did she seem concerned about the red splotches on her ivory tank top, compliments of the tropical salsa that had hit its mark, thanks to his first attack.

The floor, table and chairs were littered. Taking another calculated step in her direction, he said, "It's too bad you sent Inez home. Or do you rich people call a party service to do the cleanup?"

She lifted her chin haughtily. "You really need to try to get past the rich versus poor elements of our pasts."

He almost smiled. Oh, she was witty, articulate, cunning. And bratty. God yes, she was that, and more.

He flung a portion of the rice stuffing. The mixture scattered, part of it catching in the little hollow at the base of her neck, only to drop slowly inside the scoop neck of her top. Tripp waited with bated breath for the pieces of food to come tumbling out of the bottom edge, then spent far longer than he should have wondering precisely where those morsels had lodged. A fantasy played out in his mind. He imagined lifting her arms and peeling the shirt over her head. Her bra would come next. He would unfasten the closure and slowly lower one strap and then the other. When he'd bared her breasts he would bend down...

His body heated. Damn.

Taking advantage of his momentary lapse, Amber sprang around the table to ambush him. He caught her wrist when her hand was a matter of inches from his face.

Their eyes met. He could blame his desire on the erotic fantasies he'd been harboring, but he had no one to blame but himself for the way he brought her hand to his mouth and licked a path across her palm.

Her lips parted; her eyelashes lowered dreamily. He heard her breath hitch in her throat, and felt her shudder beneath his tongue. His overheated blood surged through him, pooling low. Dangerously low.

It had been a long time since he'd lived dangerously, since he'd let the adrenaline rushing through him guide his actions. He released her wrist, then glided his hand down her arm. Her skin was smooth, the muscles firm, yet supple. Blood pounded a pagan rhythm in his ears, and his gaze fixed on her mouth.

Her lips lifted in a smile. In a flash, he realized her intent. He made a move to grab her wrist again, but he was too late. Crème brûlée covered the lower half of his face.

She laughed out loud and spun around. He caught her by the arm and pulled her back. With his other hand, he scooped a portion of the creamy mixture from his chin with one, and only one, intention in mind.

She ducked her head and laughed again, the sound playful and mischievous and so damned musical he stopped the forward motion of his hand, suspending it in midair inches from her face. He drew her around to face him. Their gazes met, and her laughter trailed away.

Her eyes were large, her pupils dilated in the dimly lit

room. Her lashes swept down, throwing a momentary shadow on her cheeks. With their upward sweep, she rose on tiptoe. Gently, her lips touched his.

The kiss was so light it was barely a kiss at all, so brief that their eyes remained open. As she drew away, she licked her lips, tasting the concoction she'd gathered from his mouth. "This is an interesting way to sample dessert."

His body heated further, a muscle working in his throat.

"Hold that thought," she whispered. "If Perkins sees you looking at me like this, he won't question our engagement."

"Then this—" He cleared his throat. "This is part of the drill?"

Her answer was a small nod that wasn't really a nod at all. "What would you say it is?"

He would say it wasn't enough.

He flung the handful of food to the table, then cupped her shoulders, filling his hands with warm woman. Her silky tank bunched beneath his fingers as he drew her closer. "I would say," he murmured close to her lips, "that practice makes perfect."

This time their eyes closed when their lips met, their hands gliding over clothing that might never be free of food stains again. His palms smoothed down the sides of her waist, drawing her more fully against him, the entire length of her body pressed firmly to the entire length of his, his hands molding, learning, exploring.

Amber was doing some exploring of her own, her hands gliding across Tripp's shoulders. His muscles bunched and flexed beneath her palms. His breathing became ragged as her fingers inched lower. He tasted of mint and cream and smelled of dinner and deep summer. He felt like heaven.

He made a sound deep in his throat, part need, part frustration, all male. So this, she thought, was how it felt to hold a hundred and eighty pounds of tall, lean, muscular man in her arms. Never had she felt more feminine, so desirable, or so wanton.

The kiss deepened, and her breath whooshed out of her, but she didn't end the kiss. She didn't want it to end. She wanted to climb right inside this kiss, right inside this man, where she could experience this passion from the inside out.

Her initial response to him earlier in the week had been powerful, but she hadn't been prepared for the sensations swirling through her right now. She'd kissed her share of men over the years. Once, she'd even kissed a prince. But no man had ever kissed her in return in exactly this way. Certainly, no man had ever made her feel so enchanted.

Tripp's body was pressed to the front of hers. Dizzy, she realized the hard edge of the table was pressing into the backs of her thighs. Hadn't she been facing the other way when the kiss had started? He didn't give her a chance to ask. He barely gave her a chance to think. He was too busy molding her, from thigh to shoulders, to every hard inch of him. And she was too busy reveling in the scent of man, the taste of man, and the knowledge that this man wasn't immune to her scent, her taste, her touch.

Footsteps sounded behind them. Amber wouldn't have paid them any attention, nor would she have given Inez's "Oh, excuse me!" another thought, if Inez's voice had trailed away and her footsteps had faded away on tiptoe.

Those footsteps didn't fade away. They came closer,

Inez's shoes squishing on the sticky floor. Her voice rose an octave, growing louder, and so shrill Tripp and Amber jerked apart.

Inez sputtered and pointed and sputtered some more. Tripp appeared frozen. One look at his face was all it took for Amber to know that she had to think fast. She traipsed to the table, where she grabbed the linen napkins, then handed one to him. Using the other to tidy her face and hands, she smiled sweetly. "You're right. Practice does make perfect. I'd say we pretty much nailed everything from the choreography to the tilt of our heads. No need to practice it again before Saturday. It's too bad, too. That kiss wasn't half-bad."

He got that arguesome look on his face. His eyes narrowed, his lips thinned, and his jaw set. Amber turned to Inez. Her expression wasn't difficult to decipher, either. The shock was gone. In its place was an expression Amber had grown up with, letting her know in no uncertain terms that she had some explaining to do.

"I thought you'd gone, Inez."

"I came back to make sure you two hadn't started World War Three." Hands on ample hips, the short woman with the flashing brown eyes looked from one to the other. "I am too late, I think." She turned on her heel, returning moments later with a wastebasket in her hands. "Well? Do either of you have anything to say for yourselves?"

Tripp remained silent. Amber tossed the linen napkin to the table. "Tripp and I had something to settle. Don't worry, Inez. I'll clean this up." Amber turned to Tripp. "As soon as I see Tripp to the door."

Tripp glanced at Inez. She didn't smile, but she didn't look particularly angry anymore, either. She did, however, indicate, with the thrust of one shoulder, that Amber had left the room.

In his youth, Tripp would have needed to save face by having the last word. One thing life had taught him was that sometimes all a man could do was hold his head high and leave as quickly and quietly as possible.

Amber was holding the door open for him when he reached the elaborate front foyer. "You're probably still hungry," she said. "We didn't get through the main course, did we?"

Tripp ran a hand over his chin. Main course, hell. If Inez hadn't interrupted, they would have been experiencing more than dinner right now. And what the hell did she mean that kiss wasn't half-bad? It was a hell of a lot better than that. And dammit, why was he angry? "Amber—"

"I know." She pulled a face. "We'd better not try that at Alessandro's."

He stared at her, his hands curling into fists at his sides. "That's it? That's all you have to say?"

She glanced up at him, then reached up and picked a crumb from his hair. "Don't worry about helping clean up. You were my guest. Now, as far as Saturday evening goes, I think it would be best if you picked me up at my friend's house in Cloverdale. I get carsick easily, and by meeting you there, I can break up my trip. It's only a thirty-minute drive from Claire's house to Santa Rosa. I'll fax you directions."

His gaze drilled into her. Vowing to show him how unaffected she was, Amber forced an iron control she didn't feel. "Is that satisfactory?" she asked.

He studied her for a moment longer, then nodded curtly.

She absolutely, positively forbade herself to sigh in

relief. ''In that case, I'll excuse myself and help Inez with the cleanup.''

The moment he was out the door, she closed it behind him, then leaned weakly against it. Amber knew enough about body language to know when a man had something on his mind. He was undoubtedly trying to make sense of what had just happened between them. She didn't want to compartmentalize the attraction and desire they felt for each other, because she was growing more and more certain there was more to it than desire on his part, too.

All women knew that men thought, acted, and reacted differently than women. Men's bodies weren't necessarily connected to their brains. At least not when it came to sex, and certainly not when they were younger. When did men outgrow their little tendency to get turned on by the sight of any woman with a pretty face?

She caught her reflection in the mirror. There was a piece of shrimp sticking out of her hair, red splotches all over her silk tank top, and traces of orange goo streaking one cheek. That was some pretty face.

Hope fluttered inside her like butterfly wings. Maybe Tripp's reaction had to do with emotions, with feelings and a growing regard. Oh, he wanted her. Her body still burned from the way he'd pressed the physical evidence of his desire against her belly.

Whether he was ready to admit it or not, he liked her. The thing was, she liked him, too. He was difficult at times, a challenge always. Trying to stay one step ahead of him was invigorating. She hadn't been bored in days, but even she knew that this was more than a case of not being bored.

Tripp had the looks, the style and the moves to unsettle her feminine heart. The question was, did she have what it took to unsettle his?

By God, she was going to try.

* * *

Tripp eased his car around the corner on a tree-lined street on the outskirts of Cloverdale. He was early. And nervous. A double rarity for him.

Following the directions Amber had faxed to him the day before yesterday had been easy. Located on Highway 101, Cloverdale was easy to find and too small to get lost in.

Squinting against the glare of the late evening sun, he groped for his sunglasses on the seat beside him. He located them just as he spotted his second turn. According to Amber's directions, he only had a few more blocks to go. He spied her shiny red sports car in a driveway in the next block.

He slowed his car to a crawl.

Amber had mentioned that her friend Claire was an artist. Evidently, she wasn't a starving one, because her house was a large, ornate Victorian, palatial in design, and painted several shades of purple. He slid a finger between his neck and the starched collar of the shirt André had chosen. Amber had rich friends. Like drew like.

And sometimes, opposites attracted.

Damn, that was what he and Amber were: opposites who were attracted. Extremely attracted.

Tripp had heard from several reliable sources that Amber had visited the hospital in Ukiah yesterday. He'd had to take their word for it, for she hadn't bothered to stop by his office. Other than that fax, he hadn't seen or heard from her since Thursday. Perhaps if he had, he would have been able to put that kiss behind him. As it was, he couldn't get it out of his mind.

For the hundredth time, he told himself that the entire episode was a coincidence, nothing more. He'd been harboring some incredibly stimulating fantasies while partaking in that food fight, and coincidence or not, any man would have reacted to the tremble in a beautiful woman's touch, the sultriness in her voice.

That wasn't what bothered him. It was something else, and it had been bothering him even before Amber had flung that first glob of creamy goo. It was Coop who'd hit the nail on the head when he'd exclaimed how everyone in the hospital was talking about Amber Colton. "Who could miss hair that color, and eyes such a vivid shade of green? I wouldn't mind attending that dinner in Santa Rosa, just to see what she wears. She'll probably flash like a neon sign."

The description had struck a nerve, and had brought back the only useful piece of advice Tripp's old man had ever given him. "Stick with your own kind, kid. Anybody else will either leave you or die. In the end, it's all the same thing."

Tripp had been seven, and just old enough to read the marker on his mother's grave. Grace Ann Bradley had been twenty-five.

"Listen up," Randolph "Rudy" Calhoun had said to the son of the woman he'd professed to love but had never bothered to marry. "You stay away from women with skin lighter than yours. There are two kinds of white girls. The ones who think they're too good for us, and the ones who don't. The ones who don't are even more dangerous, because they go where we go. And that makes them sitting ducks and easy targets for somebody with a score to settle. That's what happened to your poor mama."

Tripp might have heeded his father's warning, if Rudy hadn't turned from his son and walked away. After that, the man had drifted in and out of Tripp's life, mostly out.

Tripp had spent the next ten years being shuffled from one relative to another—except for his time at the Hope-chest Ranch—and hating his old man for it. He'd hated a lot of people back then. That all had begun to change the summer he turned fifteen.

Tripp was one quarter Latino, but his skin was as brown as his grandfather's had been. The red-haired psychology student he'd dated in college had claimed his attraction to fair-skinned women stemmed from the fact that his mother had been fair. She'd believed it was also the reason he'd tried so hard to earn Meredith Colton's respect the summer he'd gone to live at Hacienda de Alegria.

The psychology student had left him when she'd grown bored with the thrill of the chase. That was all right. He hadn't loved her. Until Tripp met Olivia Babcock, he hadn't allowed himself the luxury of a relationship in years. That one hadn't been as disastrous as the others, but it proved he was still attracted to women completely wrong for him. Women like Amber, who, for all their beauty, would stick out in his world like a sore thumb.

He climbed out of his car, ran a hand through his hair and buttoned the middle button on his black suit. He didn't even recognize his own reflection in the car window. But he recognized the thought running through his mind. It was a vow he'd made a long time ago. No more excuses. No more coincidences. No more prolonging the inevitable. Before the night was through, he would make certain that Amber knew just how temporary this was.

Amber's breath caught in her throat at the first sight of the intense, incredibly handsome man on Claire's front porch. "You're right on time, Doctor."

"It's a first for me."

She noticed Tripp didn't smile. Holding fast to the doorknob, she moved to one side, motioning him in. He entered without saying a word.

"We have a few minutes," she said. "Would you care for a glass of wine?"

He shook his head, and she wondered if he would have preferred a shot of whiskey, straight up. She wished he would say something. A compliment would have been nice. She'd bought a new black dress for the occasion and had fixed her hair on top of her head, securing it with tiny, amber-edged pins. She'd studied her reflection for a long time, applying her makeup with a steady, light hand, placing more emphasis on her eyes than on the rest of her face. As a result, her lashes were long and thick, her lids tinted a smoky shade of gray. She'd applied tinted gloss to her lips, a bit of translucent powder to the rest of her face, and had followed that up with a touch of blush. The result was understated and elegant. It would have been nice if he'd noticed.

She glanced at Tripp and caught him staring. Oh, he'd noticed, all right. Suddenly she felt buoyant. With a lift of her brows, which she'd darkened just enough to call attention to the delicate arch, she said, "All right, then. We might as well get an early start into Santa Rosa."

She leaned around him, reaching for her beaded black bag. He took a sharp breath and finally spoke. "Little P.J. was right. You do smell good."

Her heart slowed, and a warm glow flowed through her. "P.J. said that?"

His eyes delved into hers. "Coop was wrong, though. He predicted you would wear something flashy, red and preferably low-cut."

That was what men got for making blind assumptions.

"Red," she said, leading the way to the door, "would never do. My job is to appear demure and charming at your side. Men of power, breeding and high social standing might look twice at a waitress or sales clerk wearing red, but they expect the women in their social arenas to appear in subdued, refined clothing."

"Do you rich people take classes to learn this?" He held up one hand. "I know, I know. I need to get past the rich versus poor element of our pasts."

She smiled, because dry humor was better than no humor, and Tripp's dry humor made her heart swell with feeling. "Alessandro's is an elegant restaurant. I imagine there will be other colors besides black. I chose this dress because I want to complement, not outshine. I certainly don't want to outshine Mrs. Perkins, who will probably be wearing silver, or gold lamé. And no, they don't teach this in school. Being rich isn't all fun and games. And for your information, the rules were made long before I was born."

She reached up with her right hand, touching the dark hair that caressed his collar. "It's a shame that some people place so much importance on looks. When did you have it cut?"

He stared into her eyes so long she got lost in his gaze. "This morning."

"Did it hurt?"

"Only my pride."

"I'm proud of you."

"Because I got a haircut?"

She shrugged a shoulder. He'd sacrificed so much for the kids he wanted to help. In that instant, her heart seemed to flip. When it righted itself, it pumped with new meaning. Amber was falling in love.

She felt breathless, joyful. "If it's any consolation, you

look wonderful. Your hair is short enough to appear polite and reputable and still long enough to set you apart
from the boring, civilized upper-crust men you're about
to impress.''

Tripp didn't move, not even to breathe. Amber combed
her fingers through the hair above his ears as she spoke,
the butterfly touch of her fingertips sending a heady
rhythm through his body, causing him to lose his train
of thought. His gaze did a slow glide down her body.
Her dress was long and black and sleeveless. The neck-
line was a gentle sweep from shoulder to shoulder, just
low enough to show off the delicate hollow at the base
of her neck and the soft-looking skin above her collar-
bone. The matte-black fabric skimmed over her curves,
hiding all but the barest hint of what lay underneath. It
was demure, all right; all except the slit that revealed her
slender, silk-encased leg from ankle to thigh.

"Ready?" she asked.

He nodded and, in a voice huskier than he would have
liked, said, "In case I forget later, thank you.''

She wet her lips, smiled. "Don't mention it.''

"I mean it, Amber. If I get this position, I'll be forever
indebted to you.''

"What do you mean if?''

Her smile was playful and reminded him of the way
she'd smiled just before flinging that first spoonful of
crème brûlée the other night. It caused him to add,
"Whether I get the position or not, one thing's for sure.
I'll never again be able to eat shrimp scampi or crème
brûlée without having fond memories of you.''

Since she had the key, he strode ahead of her out the
door. Therefore, he didn't see the way her smile slid off
her face as the underlying meaning in his words soaked
in.

Amber turned on a night-light, then followed more slowly, her mind a jumbled mixture of dashed hope and reality. People didn't say they would have fond memories of someone they planned to see again. People had fond memories of someone they once knew.

That was what she would be to Tripp. Someone he once knew. Someone he thought about a few times a year, perhaps less. Moments ago she'd realized she was falling in love with him. She didn't want to be someone he once knew.

If he was aware of her inner turmoil, he didn't let on during the drive to Santa Rosa. Perhaps that was because she kept up her end of the conversation, talking about her work and his. Mention of the Hopechest Ranch, where she had an office, sparked his memories of the months he'd spent there. She told him how much the place had changed in recent years. There were now between thirty and forty kids staying at the ranch at any given time. Besides the Homestead, a dormitory-style lodge where the temporary residents, as he'd been, stayed while awaiting adoption or foster homes, there was now a residence called The Shack, which was for delinquents who needed a last chance before being shipped to lock-in juvenile centers that resembled jail.

For once, Tripp did as much talking as she did, asking questions about the newly constructed "Emily's House," a home for unwed, teenage mothers. He seemed genuinely awed by her devotion to the ranch and the Hopechest Foundation she worked so hard for.

The more Amber talked about her work, the more she despaired. She felt rooted to the foundation headquarters. Okay, she had been a little bored lately, but she was needed there. It drove home the point Tripp had made earlier. Amber lived in Fort Bragg, and worked near Prosperino at the Hopechest Ranch. If Tripp acquired the position in Dr. Perkins's practice, he would live and work hours away on the other side of the mountains. It might as well have been on the other side of the world.

He needed her help to obtain that position in Santa Rosa. And she wanted to help. She did. She was only too happy to help, but in doing so, she was ensuring that their renewed acquaintance would be fleeting. By lending him her family name and influence, she was sealing the fate of their relationship and reducing it to something she feared. Temporary.

The word froze in her brain. That was what it would be—a brief interlude, passionate, perhaps, but above all else, temporary.

She didn't want this to end before it had really begun. She wanted to feel his arms go around her, to lay her head on his shoulder. She wanted to talk about mundane things, like the weather, and important things, like politics and health issues and global warming. She wanted the relationship to grow more intimate on every level.

Had it been doomed before it began?

If he was awarded that position, it was.

Whatever was a woman to do?

Maybe she should start another food fight, thereby ensuring that Tripp didn't obtain the position. She could always slurp her soup or drink from the finger bowl. Maybe she should have worn red. No, she couldn't do any of those things. Too many children's lives would be adversely affected.

Maybe they could have a long-distance relationship. But she didn't see how a long-distance relationship could ever work. She got sick every time she drove across the coastal mountains. And as a new pediatrician in a busy practice, Tripp wouldn't have time to make the trip to see her.

She wanted an up-close-and-personal relationship, not a long-distance one.

It seemed that Tripp had been right. Lies really were like dogs. They seemed harmless at first, docile, even. But later, they turned on you, attacking just when you thought you were safe.

What was she going to do?

She didn't have an answer when they pulled up in front of the restaurant in Santa Rosa. She waited for Tripp to open her door, accepted his help from the car, then took the arm he offered. While he handed the valet the keys, she pasted a smile on her face, then strode with him through the high, arched door of the most expensive and elegant restaurant in town.

Six

Tripp was only vaguely aware of the heads that turned as he made his way back toward the table in the semi-private dining alcove at Alessandro's. If he'd been looking, he would have noticed the dark-haired woman watching his every move. His only thoughts were of the questions he'd been asked and the direction the conversation had taken over dinner. All in all, it had gone quite well. A lot of it was Amber's doing.

When he'd excused himself, she'd been deep in conversation with Dr. and Mrs. Perkins. This kind of socializing came as naturally to her as treating patients came to him. Talking to Coop, worrying about his next dollar, and trying to stay out of Nurse Proctor's way came naturally to him. Schmoozing was as foreign to him as the language on the menu.

Alessandro's was everything Amber said it would be. How had she put it? Opulent grandeur at its finest. Nearly everything in the restaurant was silver-blue and white. White damask slip covers on every chair; white-blue flames flickered atop tall white tapers in silver candelabra. Waiters wearing white gloves and black tails served everything from champagne to caviar from gleaming, sterling silver trays.

Tripp had lost track of how many courses there had been. Back home, supper took fifteen minutes to cook and another fifteen to eat. Here, eating took all night.

The differences didn't end there. He'd never spent so much time eating so little, and using so many different forks to do it. He'd just run into the biggest difference. In places where he normally dined, men in tuxedoes didn't hand out towels in the men's room. If he hadn't seen the gray-haired gentleman ahead of him drop a ten-spot into a silver dish, Tripp wouldn't have remembered to tip. Rich people found the damnedest ways to spend their money.

On the bright side, he figured that if these people could spend their pocket money on human towel dispensers, there was a good chance they would be willing to part with a great deal more on medical clinics to aid the poor. If he got the position in Perkins's practice, that is.

The evening did seem to be going well, all things considered. Dr. and Mrs. Perkins were extremely friendly. He couldn't get a handle on Perkins's partners, Gentry and Harris. They and their wives remained polite and formal. Tripp would have liked to get Amber to himself for a few minutes to get her take on the evening.

Just then, two waiters stepped aside, and Tripp had a clear view of Amber. She was talking to Montgomery and Cornelia Perkins. The soft light from the crystal chandeliers turned Cornelia's perfectly coifed hair pale silver. The same light caught on the amber-colored spar-

kles in Amber's upswept hair and turned her blond
tresses the color of spun gold.

He neared the table while she was laughing at something Montgomery Perkins said. She glanced up as Tripp
approached, and it occurred to him that her smile didn't
reach her eyes.

It wasn't the first time it had happened tonight. "Having fun?" he asked quietly.

The corners of her mouth lifted. Again, the smile
didn't quite make it all the way to her eyes. He leaned
down, but before he could ask if she felt all right, Cornelia said, "I believe these young people would like to
spend time alone."

Across the table, Winston Harris said, "They're
young, Cornelia. They have plenty of time ahead of them
to be alone together."

Amber looked up at Tripp. She noticed he didn't comment one way or the other. He was the one who rarely
smiled, and yet it was getting increasingly difficult for
her to do so.

No matter what Winston Harris insinuated, she and
Tripp didn't have the rest of their lives to be together. At
best, they had a few more hours.

She'd been despairing about the situation all evening.
She hadn't slurped her fricassee or dropped her fork. She
couldn't. This was too important for Tripp, and for hundreds of children and their families who needed a doctor
like him.

She'd done her best to impress this group of pediatricians and their wives. Tripp had handled himself admi-
rably. She saw no reason on earth why Dr. Perkins would
offer the position to anyone else. She was proud of Tripp.
And sad, because her time with him was nearly over.

"There's an orchestra playing, and a small dance floor

on the other side of the room." Placing a hand on her shoulder he said, "Seems a shame to waste it."

He cocked an eyebrow, waiting for her reply. Her heart fluttered, and a delicious sensation settled low in her belly. Surely, somewhere in the dark recesses of his mind he knew exactly what he was doing. Suddenly, it seemed imperative to feel his arms go around her, if only on the dance floor. She was placing her hand in his when a deep, sultry voice she didn't recognize came from a few feet away.

"Why, hello, Dr. Perkins, Mrs. Perkins. Tripp."

"Olivia, dear," Cornelia said. "How nice to see you."

Amber glanced up just as one of the most beautiful women in all of California took Cornelia's hand. She'd seen Olivia Babcock's photograph in the society pages several times. The petite, dark-haired woman was even lovelier in person. Her hair was the color of rich coffee. The short, wispy, smart style accentuated her delicate features and large violet eyes. Her dress was the darkest shade of purple Amber had ever seen. It was the color of royalty; Olivia wore it well.

"Is Derek here, too?" Winston Harris asked a little too quickly to escape Amber's notice.

With a shake of her head and a flutter of eyelashes, Olivia bestowed her beautiful smile on everyone in turn. "Derek is on call tonight. I'm dining with Mother and Willadine Whitherspoon. You remember her late husband, don't you? Abraham headed the most renowned cancer research team at Daddy's institute."

Amber had done some name-dropping of her own tonight, but it was difficult not to admire Olivia's technique.

"Would you care to join us?" Cornelia asked.

Amber wasn't altogether comfortable with how hopeful Mary Margaret Harris and Loretta Gentry suddenly appeared. The fact that their husbands shifted uncomfortably in their chairs was even more disconcerting to Amber. Olivia couldn't have been oblivious, but she cast another perfect smile in every direction and said, "I appreciate the invitation, but Derek and I had you to ourselves last weekend. It's only fair that Tripp and his date have the same privilege this evening." She paused, looking directly at Amber. "I don't believe we've met."

"Amber Colton, Olivia Babcock." Tripp did the honors, his muscles tensing beneath Amber's hand.

"Colton," Olivia said. "That name sounds familiar."

"Her father is Joe Colton." Winston Harris provided the information. Surely Amber wasn't the only one who thought it had been delivered in a slightly caustic tone.

Montgomery and Cornelia didn't appear to be hanging on Olivia's every word, but the Harrises and Gentrys certainly were. What was going on here?

"I've heard of Joseph Colton, of course," Olivia said. "But I seem to recall a Sophie Colton, too."

"You know my sister?"

"Sophie is your sister? I heard she was in an accident."

Amber nodded. Olivia seemed so genuine. Why, she almost seemed—well, nice. If she hadn't been Tripp's former fiancée, Amber might have liked her.

"How is Sophie?"

Amber wanted to glance at Tripp, to gauge his reaction and expression. She couldn't of course, without calling attention to the tension she sensed in him. Unobtrusively placing a gentling hand over the finger that had started fiddling with his watch, Amber said, "Sophie is fine, thanks. Actually, she's very happy. She's married now and is the mother of a beautiful baby girl."

"Be sure to give her my best." Olivia exchanged a few more words with the others, then sashayed out of sight. A taut silence ensued. Wanting a moment to gather her thoughts, Amber excused herself to the powder room.

She was sitting at a flute-edged table before a beveled mirror when Olivia entered the room. Coincidence? Amber was beginning to doubt it.

Olivia's smile was friendly, though, when she said, "What a pretty dress. I just love that style."

Amber smiled.

"And black is so tried and true and unassuming. So safe."

Amber's smile wavered.

"And it hides a whole multitude of sins, doesn't it?"

Amber's hand froze in midair for but a moment. Once she'd recovered, she applied her lipstick. It gave her a perfect excuse not to reply.

"Has Dr. Perkins broken the news yet, hon?"

Hon? Olivia's dress may have been royal purple, but Amber saw red.

Olivia pretended to gasp, her hand flying to her mouth. "Oh, dear. Now I've done it, haven't I?" Her timing perfect, she waited just long enough for the implication to soak in before adding, "Just forget I slipped. It would be best if Montgomery told Tripp in his own way."

Amber replaced the top on her lipstick then dropped the tube delicately into her small beaded bag. She was proud of how perfectly unaffected her smile appeared in the mirror. "It'll be our little secret."

She closed her purse, inspected her hair, then rose to her feet. Thankful to be taller, and thus able to look down her nose at the dark-haired woman, she quietly left the room. Inside, she was fuming. Of all the condescending, arrogant, spoiled brats! No wonder Tripp had issues with rich people!

Amber was still fuming and trying not to let it show when she returned to the table. Luckily, everyone except Tripp was involved in an in-depth discussion about someone they all knew. It awarded Amber a moment to pull a face, and Tripp a moment to whisper, "I just saw Olivia heading for the rest room. Everything all right?"

She glanced around to make sure no one was listening. "She isn't as nice as she seems."

"Next you'll tell me water is wet and the sky is blue."

Joy fluttered its delicate wings in Amber's chest. She loved to laugh. Bawdy or wry, she reacted to humor. Because it was so rare, Tripp's wry humor felt like a gift. The more she came to know him, the more she wanted to know him better. She didn't want him to move downstate. She wanted him to stay right where he was so he could fall in love with her in return. But she didn't want someone less deserving to get that position, either.

"You're quiet tonight," he said. "Something's wrong."

She looked around the table again and said, "Olivia is under the impression a decision has already been made."

"Did she tell you that outright?"

Amber shrugged. "She seemed to enjoy getting the point across."

"Damn."

Her exact thought.

"Then this was all for nothing? Act two in a one-act play? We might as well leave," he said.

She recalled Olivia's condescending manner, and darn it all, it just wasn't fair. Who was it who said all things were fair in love and war? Amber looked into Tripp's brown eyes.

This was both.

The despair she'd been fighting all evening turned into determination. Laying a hand over his, she said, "It isn't over until it's over. Follow my lead."

"I can only imagine how unhappy Dr. Cooper will be to see you go," she said, as if they'd been talking about this all along. "And Nurse Proctor, the poor dear."

She paused long enough to give the other people at the table a chance to listen. Since there were few things more desirable than something somebody else wanted, she launched into a lengthy description of the people Tripp worked with and treated in Ukiah. Before long, everyone was asking him questions about his work at County General. Amber sat back and studied the level of interest. Whenever it started to wane, she launched a new topic. She talked about his patients, little P.J.'s sad plight in particular, and the progress Tripp had made with the boy's physical therapy.

"Your practices seem somewhat unconventional," Dr. Harris said.

Amber would have liked to stick out her tongue at the old curmudgeon. Tripp simply said, "It's not that I'm unconventional. Sometimes getting to the root of a problem requires some imaginative investigation. A case in point is a little girl I've been treating. Her mother brought her to me earlier this week. Her symptoms were baffling. Lethargy, headache, muscle soreness, loss of appetite, weight loss and abdominal pain."

"Fever?" Montgomery Perkins asked.

"It came and went. I ruled out the obvious illnesses such as appendicitis and strep throat."

"A deeper, more serious illness? Leukemia, perhaps?"

Tripp shook his head. "She tested negative."

"Some sort of virus?" Steven Gentry asked, leaning ahead, elbows resting on the table.

"I considered the possibility," Tripp said, his voice deep-timbered and clear. "She was anemic, too. And irritable. It just didn't feel like a virus to me."

Now Winston Harris leaned in, too. "Did you hospitalize her?"

Tripp nodded, and Amber relaxed.

"One day I watched her, undetected. And even though she remained lethargic, she scraped halfheartedly at the paint on her bedstand."

Montgomery Perkins was the first to begin to nod. "Did you test her serum lead levels?"

A light seemed to come on in the other two doctors' eyes.

Again Tripp nodded. "I ordered the test, then made a house call, and sure enough, the paint around the windows was chipping."

"Lead poisoning," Winston Harris said. "I once treated a little boy for that. His toxicity level was dangerously high. Almost fifty micrograms cc."

"How would you rate his recovery?" Tripp asked. Now his elbows were on the table, too.

The men tossed words like erythrocyte protoporphyrin and chelation therapy into the conversation. Mrs. Harris and Mrs. Gentry exchanged resigned looks. Cornelia Perkins said, "It was inevitable that they would talk shop before the night was through."

"It's one of the plights of being a doctor's wife," Loretta said.

"You'll see, Amber," Cornelia said.

Amber had to force a smile. Inside, she despaired all over again. It was highly unlikely that she would ever know how it felt to be Tripp's wife. Regardless of the outcome of the evening, their time together was nearly over.

"Have you and Tripp set a date?" Cornelia asked.

Amber had to think fast. Taking the advice she'd given Tripp, she hovered as close to the truth as possible. "I've always thought an autumn wedding would be lovely."

"Weddings are lovely no matter what the season," Cornelia said. "Our second son is getting married in Mississippi next weekend. And it'll likely be hotter than Hades there in July."

Montgomery Perkins stopped in the middle of what he'd been saying. It was as if hearing his wife's mention of the upcoming wedding flipped a light on over his head. "I have a confession to make." He looked almost apologetic. "We thought we'd made up our minds and had chosen the candidate who would best suit our practice. Now I wish I had a little more time to make a decision. I just had an idea. Cornelia, dear, would it be possible to invite both candidates to David's wedding next weekend?"

"Why, I don't know…"

"That is," Montgomery said, peering from Tripp to Amber, "if the two of you can make it on such short notice. I'll invite Derek and Olivia, too." He rubbed his hands together. "Why, I don't know why I didn't think of this sooner. It'll kill two birds with one stone. Pardon the expression. We'll get better acquainted with both couples in an entirely different setting. Then we'll be able to make an educated decision based on more than a few brief encounters."

Winston Harris opened his mouth to speak, then seemed to think better of it. Poor Cornelia was still gasping, too, one plump hand fluttering to the gold lamé collar on her gown. "I'll have to call Jennifer's mother, and make certain it's acceptable." The lovely, sixty-something-year-old woman recovered slightly. "If it's acceptable to the bride's family, I see no reason not to second the invitation."

"The wedding is in Mississippi, you said?" Amber asked.

"Yes. It's going to be held in Jennifer's parents' home. It's a lovely, stately, antebellum mansion between Vicksburg and Jackson. It's positively stunning."

"Is that a problem?" Montgomery asked.

"Of course not," Amber said. Oh, my, she thought. That meant she would have to fly.

She looked at Tripp, and he said, "I'll try to get one of the doctors to cover for me at the hospital."

"Then it's settled," Montgomery exclaimed. "As soon as Cornelia clears it with our future daughter-in-law, we'll contact you so you can make arrangements. I'll call Derek and Olivia, too."

The party broke up soon after. Amber's daze didn't lift until she and Tripp reached the Cloverdale village limit. Her time with Tripp wasn't over, and neither was their pretend engagement. The charade would continue.

She was thrilled and relieved and scared to death. She'd fallen in love with a man with brawn and brains and might and morals. She had one more week with him. Could he fall in love with her in that time? If he did, what then?

It would be worse if he didn't.

One week wasn't much time, but it was a week longer than she thought she would have. She vowed to use it wisely.

Amber gave the door of her father's study a quick rap with her knuckles, then turned the handle and quickly poked her head inside. "Hi, Daddy, it's me."

She stopped abruptly, because her father wasn't sitting behind his huge mahogany desk. Her mother was.

Amber's spontaneous smile gave way to a much more practiced one. "Mother. Hello. Where is everybody?"

"How would I know?" Meredith Colton snapped. "Nobody in this household listens to a word I say. It's a disgrace, the shape it's in."

Eyeing the wall of bookshelves on the opposite wall, the cabinets and desktop, every surface freshly polished, Amber disagreed. The house was lovely, the floors so clean a person could eat off them. She remembered the food fight she and Tripp had. Biting her lip at the memory, she said, "Where's Dad?"

"He isn't here."

She could see that, but she'd experienced her mother's wrath firsthand far too often to point out that fact. Treading lightly, she said, "What are you doing here, Mother?"

"This is my home."

"Of course. I didn't mean... That is..." Amber could feel her throat closing up. She and her mother couldn't even be in the same room anymore without the skin on the back of Amber's neck prickling. "I didn't know you were home. How are you, Mother?"

"I'm fine. I see you haven't had time for a facial lately. You really shouldn't neglect your skin."

A sadness so deep it had eaten a hole through Amber's insides years ago started to ache. What happened? They used to be so close.

This woman felt like a stranger to her.

"Do you know where Dad went?"

"Your father is away on business. Where doesn't mat-

ter. He won't be back for several days." She might as
well have added, "Thank God." It was there in her voice
and in her eyes.

"Oh. Well, I mean… That is…"

"Amber, please don't stammer. And stand up
straight."

Since arguing got her nowhere with the woman, Amber sighed and did as her mother said. "I just stopped by
to tell Dad goodbye."

"You're leaving?"

Amber thought her mother could at least pretend to be
sorry to see her go. "I'm going to Mississippi for the
weekend."

"Why? Why on earth would you go there?"

Amber looked closer at her mother. Why the sudden
interest in Amber's whereabouts? Or was it the destina-
tion that was causing her mother's concern?

"Tripp and I are attending a wedding there."

The other woman visibly relaxed. "Take plenty of hair
gel. The humidity wreaks havoc with a woman's hair."

Hair gel. That was what their relationship had been
reduced to. Facials, good posture and hair gel.

Her mother didn't ask about Tripp, or how flying
would affect Amber. Amber wished her father had been
here. She missed him and had wanted to see him before
she left tomorrow. He, at least, would have been interested in what she did, where she went. Feeling sad that
she couldn't reach through the brittle veneer to the warm
heart of the mother she once knew, Amber said, "Will
you tell Daddy I stopped by? And tell him I'm sorry I
missed him."

"I'll be sure to relay the message."

* * *

Like hell she would, Patsy thought after that little do-gooder left the room. She hated being called Mother by Meredith's children. She hated being called Meredith even more. Perhaps some day she could reclaim her real name. Until then, she must continue the charade.

Patsy eyed the telephone. She was waiting for a call from Silas Pike.

She shuddered. The man, with his grimy ponytail and Fu-Manchu mustache and goatee, was as inept as he was ugly. He'd screwed up too many times to count. But he was the only person Patsy had been able to find to finish the job that car accident had started ten years ago.

Patsy sighed. Turning in Joe's oversized leather chair, she watched as Amber drove out of the driveway in her smart little sports car. Patsy had sent everyone on errands this morning, and had thought she had the house to herself. She must have been in her room when Amber arrived. Now, Patsy thought, the coast was clear for her meeting with Silas Pike.

His phone call was late, and Patsy's stomach was in knots. Seeing Amber hadn't helped. It never did. Everyone said that both Amber and Sophie looked just like her. Amber, especially, with her sunny personality and quick sense of humor acted so much like Meredith it turned Patsy's stomach.

Patsy had resented her twin sister all her life. Being forced to be nice to Amber, who acted just like her mother, was more than Patsy should have been forced to endure.

She'd already endured so much. Since the very beginning, everything had gone awry. She'd been treated unfairly all her life, the downtrodden twin, while Meredith was doted upon. The fact that they were identical didn't seem to matter to their mother, who'd placed Meredith on a pedestal while finding fault with everything Patsy did. She hated her mother for that. She hated Meredith most of all. Amber wasn't much better. She reminded Patsy too much of Meredith. Sophie, too. Why couldn't Joe and Meredith's children just leave and never come back? Was that too much to ask?

But no, even grown up, they came back time and time again. With their every return, Patsy was forced to remember Meredith. And she wanted to forget her identical twin sister had ever existed.

Besides, no matter what anybody said, neither Amber nor Sophie worked as fastidiously at their looks as Patsy did, therefore neither of them were as stunning as she was. Of course, it cost a pretty penny to keep up features like hers. Her hair stylist, manicurist, masseuse and clothing experts were the best money could buy. She was worth it. She deserved all the special treatment. Why, what with everything she'd been forced to endure these past ten years, she deserved all this and more.

Ten long years she'd been waiting, suffering through this charade. If only Meredith had died in that car accident. Then Patsy could have assumed Meredith's identity without all these headaches. Without always fearing the worst. Without constantly looking over her shoulder, worrying that Meredith might return at any moment. Without wondering if that plain little red-headed brat, Emily, whom Meredith and Joe were stupid enough to adopt, might show up here with someone who believed her story of seeing two mothers at the accident. Once, Patsy had overheard Emily, the simpering little orphan, refer to her as the bad mommy.

What if somebody believed her story? What then?

Patsy had had no choice but to hire Silas "Snake Eyes" Pike to silence Emily once and for all. Patsy was supposed to get rid of Joe at the same time. Could nothing ever go smoothly?

With Joe gone, and Meredith and Emily out of the way, Patsy would have had all the Colton money. Then she could raise her darlings, Joe, Jr. and Teddy. And she could use every means to find the baby girl she'd lost so many years ago.

Patsy massaged her temples. She wanted the perfect life she'd always dreamed of. Soon, she told herself.

Silas insisted he was getting closer to discovering Emily's whereabouts. And as inept as he was, the other P.I. she'd hired to find her twin was probably right about the fate Meredith had undoubtedly met. It was comforting to believe that Meredith had become a homeless person with no memory, and more than likely, died as a Jane Doe. It was fitting. Patsy liked to imagine it that way.

She leaned back in Joe's chair, continuing to wait for Silas Pike to call. The phone didn't ring, but at least the new gardener she'd hired pulled into the driveway. No matter how much she'd badgered him, Marco Ramiriz had refused to rid the gardens of the pitiful plants Meredith had grown years ago. Patsy would see that the new gardener did as she said. After all, it wouldn't require a green thumb to yank out plants that shouldn't have survived to begin with.

Bit by bit, year by year, she was ridding her life of everything Meredith had touched. She would enjoy watching the destruction of the few remaining wildflowers and scraggly plants Meredith had once loved. The anticipation made her smile.

The phone rang. Her smile turned nasty the instant she

heard the sound of Silas Pike's voice on the other end. He was sniveling. She hated sniveling. She'd hired him to put an end to the problem of Emily Blair once and for all. He was inept. She hated that most of all. He'd been so close to finding that little brat who could at any moment insist that she, Patsy, wasn't who she said she was. Emily, with her sickening nickname, "Sparrow," was a loose end that needed to be eliminated.

"I don't want to hear any more excuses," Patsy said in a low, menacing voice.

She rolled her eyes as Silas spouted several more reasons that he hadn't been successful this far.

"Just keep a watchful eye on that do-gooder Wyatt Russell and his new little wife, Annie. While you're at it, keep close tabs on Toby Atkins. I have a feeling he knows more about Emily's whereabouts than a good sheriff should."

Silas made noises about needing money.

"I've given you all the money you're going to get this month. Lay off the booze, and find Emily. And when you do, await my instructions."

She hung up. Looking out the window again, she tried to cheer herself with the knowledge that one day soon, all this unpleasantness would be behind her, and this entire estate would be hers.

"Louise?"

The beautiful woman finished snipping the flower from its delicate stem before glancing at Martha Wilkes, who watched Louise closely as she neared.

In a soft, Southern accent, Martha said, "You still aren't comfortable answering to that name, are you?"

For ten years she'd been going by the name Louise

Smith. She shrugged and did her best to smile. She didn't believe for a moment she was fooling Dr. Martha Wilkes.

"Do you still want to go through with the meeting with Emily and Rand, who claim you're their long-lost mother?"

Yes! No! Yes. She was terrified. According to her records, her past wasn't pretty. Patsy Portman. That was the name on her file. It felt as unnatural as Louise Smith. There was something vaguely familiar about Portman, but she couldn't imagine being called Patsy.

Once, in a dream, she'd heard someone call her name. When she awoke, she remembered the dream, but not her own real name. It was an M word, like Mary, or Marianne, or Mary Beth. Or perhaps what she'd heard was Mommy.

Massaging her temples to stave off the headache that invariably accompanied probing too deeply into her memory, Louise considered telling Martha to cancel the meeting. Then she would go running into her home, where she could hide from the nightmares that had haunted her for ten long years. She might have succumbed to the hysteria that threatened to overwhelm her. But she didn't, because not all her dreams had been unpleasant. Sometimes, she felt a sense of déjà vu so powerful she was faint and hopeful at the same time. There was a place deep inside her, a place beyond logic and reason, that had experienced a great love, and children's laughter, and tears, and joy. Other doctors and therapists she'd seen over the years had dismissed the sensation, theorizing that it was most probably due to the fact that she'd once given up an infant for adoption. For a long time Louise had accepted that explanation. But that theory couldn't explain the visions she'd been having of a tall, dark man. In her most recent dreams, he'd stood in a lush garden, surrounded by children of all ages, all waiting expectantly for her, arms open wide, as if waiting for her to come home. The garden in her dreams was similar to the garden she was standing in right now including a fountain. But that garden and fountain were larger, and there was a swimming pool, and a sound that could only be the ocean carrying on a soft breeze.

Where was the garden of her dreams? Who was the man? And who were the children who called out to her but she couldn't quite hear?

She looked into the distance where the sun glinted off the wings of a jet cutting through a cloud shaped like a turtle. Nerves tap-danced in her stomach, and a yearning so strong she nearly cried out washed over her. Oh, how she wished that man in her dreams, or one of the children, perhaps, was on that jet and was coming to invite her home.

Wherever that might be.

Louise was terrified that this girl, Emily, would take one look at her face, only to turn away, mistaken. Louise was almost as terrified that Emily wouldn't turn away, mistaken. What if Louise regained her memory, only to discover that her dreams were simply that? Dreams. What if the man didn't exist? What if his love never had?

What if she regained her memory, only to discover that she had no one?

"Louise?" Martha Wilkes placed her brown hand over Louise's pale one. "We can wait if you want to, or if you need to."

She gazed into Martha's warm, compassion-filled eyes. Taking a deep breath, she glanced at the sky. The jet was gone, and the cloud that had looked like a turtle was now just another cloud. It reminded her how much everything could change in the blink of an eye.

She knew better than anybody that life rarely handed out second chances. No matter how terrified she was, she couldn't pass up hers. "Bring Emily and her brother to me. I'll be waiting."

Seven

The air outside the airport in Jackson, Mississippi, smelled faintly of exhaust fumes and felt like deep summer. Tripp tried to help the porter stash his carry-on and all four of Amber's suitcases in the trunk of the cab. After getting in the way a few times, he stepped aside and let the man do his job. Placing a tip into the porter's open hand, Tripp climbed into the back seat next to Amber, sputtering, "I could buy a month's supply of medicine for the clinic with what I've spent on travel alone so far this weekend."

"Dr. Perkins told you to keep track of your expenses."

"I prefer to pay my own way."

She leaned ahead, speaking through a window in the glass partition. Seconds after she gave the driver directions to the bed-and-breakfast Dr. Perkins's assistant had reserved for them, the cab was speeding around winding lanes, leaving the airport behind.

"Montgomery Perkins and his associates can afford it, Tripp."

"Dammit, that isn't the point."

The taxi driver made a square turn out of a round corner. Tripp noticed the way Amber placed a hand over her stomach. She turned her head slowly and blinked, her throat convulsing on a swallow. "I'm still groggy from the airsickness pills. What are we arguing about again?"

For all the floundering he did through his mind searching for a reply, he couldn't come up with anything of value. Why was he trying to pick a fight?

And then the answer came, unbidden.

He could think of only two activities that would cure him of the unholy case of unspent desire he'd been battling ever since Amber had fallen asleep with her head on his shoulder an hour into the flight. The numbness had left his hand shortly after she'd awakened, and for the most part, the kink had worked its way out of his neck, but he hadn't forgotten how soft her hair had been beneath his cheek. And he swore her scent had permanently permeated his senses. Okay, arguing wasn't his first choice. However, it was a hell of a lot safer than the other activity.

He reminded himself that they were simply pretending to be engaged. His brain knew the difference between playacting and the real thing. Why, then, did his desire feel so real?

Because it *was* real, dammit.

Which meant that not all of this was pretend, after all. And that made it even more dangerous.

The first thing he was going to do when he got to his room was take a cold shower. Perhaps when he'd put a little distance between him and Amber he would be able to concentrate on what he would say and how he would stomach being in the same room with Derek Spencer.

Beside him, Amber was fumbling around inside her large leather purse. Bringing a pack of mints from the bottom, she offered a piece to him. "It's wintergreen," she said. "It helps soothe an upset stomach."

Her need for something to soothe her upset stomach reminded him of everything she was doing for him. She'd braved airsickness for him. She was using her vacation time for him.

Watching as she popped a mint into her mouth, he said, "You're a real trooper."

"For a spoiled little rich girl, you mean?"

She looked up at him with dewy eyes and a soft, serene smile he wouldn't have minded sampling. "You're not so spoiled. And you're a lot tougher than I gave you credit for."

Amber didn't know what she'd expected, but it wasn't a compliment, or the barely-there smile on Tripp's mouth. It certainly wasn't the whisper-soft kiss he placed on her cheek. Holding perfectly still, she closed her eyes. There was something incredible about the brush of a man's lips on a woman's cheek. It was something few men bothered with in this day and age. She doubted it was something Tripp did every day. Which made it even more special, and completely endearing.

She waited to see what he would do next. She would have loved it if he covered her mouth with his, but she wasn't entirely disappointed when he shifted to his own half of the back seat and looked out the window. There would be plenty of time for kissing once they reached the inn. Her imagination running wild with what she hoped would happen after they took their time kissing, she let her gaze trail out the window, too.

Still a little woozy, she felt airy and hopeful, too, and had even before the jet had touched down. She couldn't explain it, except that she felt close to something or someone precious. It probably had a lot to do with the man sitting next to her. But it also had to do with the dream she'd had on the plane.

She'd dreamed of her mother. Not the way her mother was now, but of how she'd been a long time ago, when Sophie and Amber and Emily had been young girls and their mother had shown them how to make flower chains in the garden near the pool. The sisters had worn them in their hair, pretending to be forest sprites and laughing until their sides hurt. Amber could still hear her mother's voice as she'd insisted the girls reminded her of birds. That day, four-year-old Emily, with her flyaway red hair and her knobby knees, had become Sparrow. Ten-year-old, golden-haired Amber was nicknamed Finch, and beautiful, lithe, twelve-year-old Sophie was Lark. Amber and Sophie had outgrown their nicknames in no time, but little Emily's had stuck.

It had been months since any of them had called Emily anything. Sparrow, Amber thought, where are you?

The taxi was idling at a red light when Amber's gaze was inexplicably drawn to a girl standing at the corner. The girl's back was to Amber, but her hair was the exact color of Emily's. Amber's heart sped up then slowed down. The girl was thinner than Amber had ever seen Emily, but her height was right, and that hair...

Amber held her breath as the girl turned. Just then, the wind blew that mane of red hair across her face, hiding it from view. Amber's hand went to the door handle. "Emily?" she called through the open window.

The sound was lost beneath revving engines and honking horns. The light had turned green and the traffic started forward.

Her heart in her throat, Amber strained to see the girl's face as they passed. But a group of tourists stepped in front of her, swallowing her into the crowd.

"Amber, what is it?"

She heard Tripp's voice, but she didn't take her eyes off that group of tourists. "See that girl? The one with the red hair?"

They both peered out the back window. "I see several girls back there. Two of them have red hair."

Amber stared wordlessly until the little entourage disappeared from view. Emotions welled in her throat. Biting her lip to keep it from quivering, she said, "I thought I saw my sister, Emily."

"Emily?" Tripp asked. "What would your adopted sister be doing in Jackson, Mississippi?"

Fighting through the cobwebs left over from her motion-sickness medicine, Amber shook her head and sighed. "You're right. What could Emily possibly be doing here?"

But where else could she be? And why hadn't she called?

They turned another corner. Before long, the cab was taking a ramp leading to a freeway. According to the directions she'd received from Dr. Perkins's assistant, Amber and Tripp were less than half an hour away from the inn.

"The journey's been hard on you," Tripp said, close to her ear. "We'll be arriving at the inn soon." He glanced at the watch he'd been fiddling with. "It looks like you'll have time to lie down for a little while when you get to your room. I brought some medical journals to read in mine."

Amber didn't say anything. Luckily, Tripp didn't glance at her. Therefore, he didn't see the smile of anticipation that settled on her mouth. And he didn't hear her murmur under her breath, "All's fair in love and war."

It wasn't fair! Emily Blair Colton thought as she stepped out of the shadows between two buildings in one of several historic districts in Jackson, Mississippi.

Homesickness washed over her. She wanted to follow that taxicab, to call out to her big sister. *Amber, come back. Don't leave me. Please.*

But Emily couldn't do that. Amber didn't know she was here. Only Rand knew. Emily hoped. The fewer people who knew where she was, the better.

She looked over her shoulder, studying every person on foot, in parked cars. Fear. She shook with it. It was so real, she could taste it. She wanted to go home. She needed to go home. That need welled up inside her, bringing tears to her eyes. Dashing them away, she prayed it would all be over soon.

Emily had the world's best reason to be in Mississippi. But what was Amber doing here? Driving great distances made her sick; flying did her in.

Peering into the distance where that taxicab had been, Emily forced her heart back into its rightful place in her chest, and wet her dry lips. She was so tired of running, so tired of being scared. She was twenty years old, far too young to feel so weary.

The past year had been a nightmare. But in reality, the nightmare had begun ten years ago, when she and her mother, the real Meredith Colton, had been in a car accident. Nothing had been truly right since.

For ten long years, Emily had tried to make sense of a hazy, out-of-focus image of her good mother being re-

placed by an evil one. And now, finally, it was all beginning to become clear, for recently, Emily's oldest
brother, Rand, had sent word to her in the little town in
Montana, where she'd been hiding. It seemed the private
investigator Rand had hired had finally found proof that
Emily's dream of seeing two mothers at the accident
scene hadn't been a hallucination. Emily's dear mother,
Meredith, had an identical twin sister named Patsy Portman. Patsy was the evil twin in every sense of the word.
Emily hadn't known she had an aunt. Rand hadn't, either.
Emily didn't begin to understand why their mother hadn't
told them of her twin sister's existence. She must have
had good reason. Perhaps one day soon they would have
answers, too.

Patsy had caused that accident. Emily was sure of that
much. Then she'd assumed Meredith's identity.

Emily didn't know why Patsy would do something so
horrible to her only sister, but at least the truth was finally
close at hand. In her heart of hearts, Emily had always
known that something had been gravely wrong with her
mother since that accident. Now, Rand had discovered
the whereabouts of the real Meredith Colton. Evidently,
their poor mother was suffering from amnesia and had
taken the name Louise Smith. Rand had already paid a
visit to her therapist, Dr. Martha Wilkes. He'd wanted to
take the situation by storm. Emily smiled, because that
was the way of most of the men in the Colton clan.

Dr. Wilkes had instructed Rand to go slowly and pro-
ceed with caution. Evidently, their mother had been having dreams for years. Sometimes they were so terrifying
they brought on horrible headaches and setbacks in her
treatment. Dr. Wilkes had told Rand that other times their
mother dreamed of a faceless man and children calling

her name. That dream always left their mother sad and lonely.

Emily understood that sadness and loneliness.

It was Dr. Wilkes's belief that the key to unlocking Meredith's memory lay in the hands of the red-haired little girl Meredith repeatedly dreamed of. Emily blinked back more tears. Her dear mother hadn't forgotten her, at least not in her heart where memories often burrowed, or in her dreams where they were relived.

Although she hadn't been born a Colton, Emily understood Rand's desire to bring their mother home. Emily, too, yearned for the love of the mother none of them had seen in ten years. That yearning had driven Emily to flee Red River in the middle of the night, hitching a ride across six states. It was a dangerous way to travel, but the real danger lay in the possibility that Patsy might discover her whereabouts. That woman was evil. Even though the past year had been hell, and she feared for her life, Emily would do it all again for the opportunity to gaze into her mother's loving face once again.

She stepped into the intersection and stuck out her thumb, only to pull it back again when an unsavory-looking man with dirty hair, a scraggly beard and grease-stained clothes slowed down. No matter how tired, or how anxious she was, she'd come too far to throw all caution to the wind now.

Hungry, thirsty and bone weary, she drew a map of Jackson from the back pocket of her jeans. As near as she could tell, she was two miles from the place where she was to meet Rand. Taking a deep breath, she tucked the map back into her pocket and her hair beneath her baseball cap. She hoisted her bag over her shoulder and headed across town.

* * *

"Martha tells me you're married?"

Emily heard Rand's sigh all the way from her side of the small garden table. "Yes," he said, to the beautiful woman that neither of them could take their eyes off, and who obviously viewed them as strangers.

Those first few moments when Emily, Rand and their mother had come face-to-face again after all these years had been awkward. Emily was tearful and frustrated. She'd fantasized about this reunion for years. In her day-dreams, her beloved mother always instantly recognized her. She did not stare at her with a distant, troubled expression. Emily had wanted to throw herself into her mother's arms. Rand, who rarely showed any emotion, had cleared his throat and tugged at his collar. Their mother's eyes had remained dry.

To her, they were strangers.

No, Emily screamed inside her head. She and Rand were her children, and not her only two. Emily had come so far, had hoped for so much, yearned for so long. She wanted to cry. Dr. Martha Wilkes gave her head the barest shake, giving both Emily and Rand a stern look. She'd warned them that it might take a while for this woman she called Louise to remember.

"My wife's name is Lucy." Rand shifted in his wicker chair, clenched and unclenched his fingers.

Meredith and Joe Colton's firstborn, Rand was an overachiever. As an attorney, he was accustomed to taking charge, being in control, getting things done. Emily thought this sitting back and waiting must be killing him. She understood his frustration and his disappointment. Rand looked so much like his father. She'd been sure their mother would take one look at him and remember everything.

"A pretty name," Meredith—Emily refused to think of her as Louise—said.

"She's incredible," Rand said. "I'd love the two of you to meet. Some time. Someday. That is…" Again, he tugged at his collar. "When you're ready. When everything finally gets back to normal."

Emily could have kissed her big brother for saying "when," and not "if."

Meredith's gaze flickered around the table, alighting on each of them for but a moment. Her beautiful brown eyes were blank, fearful almost and somehow sad. Emily was beyond words. Luckily, Rand had his wits about him. "Lucy has a five-year-old son," he said in an obvious effort to keep the conversation going. "His name is Max. Wait until you meet him."

There was something familiar about the way Meredith fingered a fold in her inexpensive, though lovely dress. There was gray in her hair now, and a few lines in her pretty face. She was no less beautiful than she'd ever been. And inside, she was the same woman who had taken one look at the toddler with the flyaway red hair, tattered dress and scraped knees, and loved her. From that day forward, Meredith had accepted Emily as her own.

There had to be a way to reach her, to help her remember.

"Rand is in the process of adopting Max, Mom," Emily said. "The way you and Dad adopted me."

Meredith's gaze caught on Emily, studying her face, as if searching for a hint of something she might remember. Birds twittered in the small, lush garden. Bees buzzed around a fence covered with honeysuckle in full bloom near the back of the property. Without taking her eyes off her mom, Emily said, "This garden reminds me of how the one at home in Prosperino used to look when you were tending it.''

It was Dr. Wilkes who said, ''That would explain why you've always been so drawn to plants more native to California than Mississippi, Louise.''

Meredith nodded. ''I've dreamed of a garden, lush and large, and of people, faceless for the most part, and voices and laughter. And I've always suspected that the sound I heard in the background was the ocean.'' She put a hand to her forehead, as if her head was beginning to throb.

Martha Wilkes reached over. ''Don't try to force it, Louise. It'll come back to you when you're ready. It might return one memory at a time, or it could return in one fell swoop.''

Meredith wavered a small smile at her therapist. Emily knew she would be forever grateful to the lovely, dark-skinned woman for the care she bestowed on her mother.

''All these years,'' her mother said in a voice so quiet both Emily and Rand had to lean forward to hear, ''I've been terrified my memory would never return. Sometimes I was almost as afraid it would, because I was pretty sure I wouldn't like the woman the clinic said I was. But I'm not her.''

She cringed at the shooting pain in her head.

''Would you like to lie down?'' Dr. Wilkes asked.

Meredith blinked. Laying both hands flat on the table, she said, ''No. What I'd like to do is serve tea.'' She glanced around, as if suddenly shy. ''Would either of you care for some?''

Emily doubted that her mother understood why she and Rand both grinned suddenly. Rand was strictly a coffee drinker, strong and black. Normally, Emily preferred cola.

Both said, "I would love some tea."

Their mother hadn't changed. She was still kind, warm, welcoming. And she still served tea this time of the afternoon.

Emily and Rand gazed longingly at her until she disappeared inside her little house. The moment she was out of hearing range, Rand began firing questions at Dr. Wilkes.

"Is there anything wrong with her besides her loss of memory?"

Before Martha could answer, Emily said, "She seems frail."

"She gets headaches, oftentimes severe. She may seem fragile, but I've witnessed her strength time and time again."

Rand nodded. "A weaker woman would have given up."

Emily said, "I always knew that if Mom was alive, she would fight to find her way back to us."

Martha nodded sagely.

"I understand how Patsy could have caused that car accident, then switched places with Mother," Rand said. "But how did Mom come to live here?"

Martha Wilkes looked at Rand with unblinking eyes so brown they appeared black. "According to the report I received from the private investigator you hired, Louise—or should I say Meredith, your mother—had somehow turned up at a clinic in Monterey. She was suffering from amnesia, but her driver's license said her name was Patricia Portman. Patsy Portman was a former patient of theirs. Your mother spent six months there. Knowledge of her supposed mental disability and her prison record must have been a horrible blow to her self-esteem. All this time, her therapists, myself included, have believed she was suffering from multiple personality disorder. Your Patsy fooled us all.''

Rand jerked to his feet and paced to an arbor covered with roses. Patsy Portman was his aunt, but he hated her with a ferocity that staggered even him. ''The thought of my mother…'' he had to clear his throat before he could continue ''The thought of her believing those morbid lies all these years, and living here, so far from the people she loved and who love her, turns my stomach.''

''I can see that.''

The straightforward reply reminded Rand that Dr. Wilkes was a very talented therapist. She was still their best bet in finding the fragile string and strumming it in a manner that would bring Meredith's memory back.

He glanced around him, ran a hand through his dark hair. ''I still can't believe how much this yard looks like the gardens at Hacienda de Alegria. It's amazing when you think about it. And fitting. Look at what she made out of nothing. She may not remember us, but inside she's the same person she always was. There has to be a way to trigger her memory.''

Emily remained quiet, listening, thinking. Wondering. Without conscious thought, she jumped to her feet and started for the house.

''Where are you going?''

She stopped suddenly. Glancing over her shoulder at the beautiful woman with smooth black skin and short, cropped hair, she turned slowly and said, ''I always helped Mom make tea.''

The therapist started to shake her head slowly.

Holding up one hand, Emily said, ''I won't do or say anything to upset her. I promise.''

She glanced to Rand. Before he opened his mouth, Dr. Wilkes said, ''I'm on to you, girl. You want your brother to distract me so you can make a run for it. Go ahead. Help your mother. But remember, I'm holding you to that promise.''

Emily twirled around again, the simple summer dress she'd changed into in Rand's hotel room tangling around her legs. Behind her, she heard her brother say, ''When this is over, we're taking you out on the town.''

Dr. Wilkes said, ''I can't remember the last time I brushed the dust off my high heels and went out on the town.''

''Well, get out your dusting cloth, because when Mom finally goes home, my father is going to want to throw a party. And he'll want you and your husband to attend.''

Martha didn't bother telling this sharp young attorney that she'd never taken the time for things like husbands or flights to California. She hadn't even dated since she was much, much younger. Now she was forty-five, and her biological clock had stopped ticking. She hoped she was never sorry.

The door closed behind Emily. Beyond the window, Martha could see Louise—no, her name was Meredith—moving about her kitchen. Her children wanted to take her home. And sooner or later, she would go. And Martha would move on to try to help her next patient.

This was the life she'd chosen. And she wasn't sorry.

''Where are you going?'' Rand asked.

Martha turned in nearly the same place Emily had moments earlier. Smiling warmly, Martha said, ''Let's go see if your mother and sister need any help with that tea, shall we?''

''Mama?''

Louise—or Meredith, or...Lord, she didn't even know what to call herself anymore—looked up from the jar where she stored her tea bags. The sight of the lovely, red-haired young woman standing in the doorway took her breath away. Or had being called "Mama" done that?

"Yes?"

Emily moved closer slowly, shyly. "I see green is still your favorite color."

Meredith looked at the green curtains she'd made herself and at the moss green walls she'd painted her kitchen. Green was her favorite color now. She hadn't known it was always the case. Motioning to the girl's dark green dress, she said, "Is it your favorite color, too?"

Emily shook her head sadly. "I like it, but my favorite is blue. Amber loves yellow, and Sophie likes red." Steadily moving closer, she said, "I thought you might like some help. Where do you keep the tray?"

"In this cabinet." Gesturing to a low shelf, Meredith leaned down. But Emily beat her there, going blithely to her haunches.

A sense of déjà vu washed over Meredith. She straightened, her heart in her throat. She didn't know why she reached a hand to gently touch a lock of Emily's hair. The young woman tilted her face up, her blue eyes delving Meredith's. There was moisture in those eyes as she reached for Meredith's hand. "Oh, Mama, don't you remember me at all?"

Meredith was rocked by a powerful wave of emotion. It was more than a flashback. It was as if some vital electric link between her conscious mind and her dormant memory had been jump-started and was pushing outward, like a seed coming to life.

Staring deeply into Emily's face from this angle, she caught a glimpse of the red-haired little girl who had haunted her dreams and had given her a reason to go on. Tears coursed down Meredith's face as she clasped Emily's hand and drew her to her feet. "Yes, I do remember you... Sparrow."

For the first time in ten long, lonely years, Emily flung herself into her mother's arms. "Oh, Mama, I've missed you so!"

A movement in the doorway drew Meredith's gaze. As if seeing the dark-haired young man for the first time, she whispered, "Joe?"

She staggered, and Rand and Martha rushed forward.

The tea kettle whistled. Meredith covered her ears and closed her eyes. In a daze, she felt herself being lowered into a kitchen chair. When she was certain she wouldn't faint, she opened her eyes. Slowly, she reached a hand to her firstborn son.

"Of course, you couldn't be Joe. You're Rand, aren't you?"

There wasn't a dry eye in the place. Emily sobbed openly. Rand's eyes swam. Martha sniffled, although she would probably never admit it out loud. Bristling, she bustled to the stove and lifted the tea kettle off the burner.

The horrendous whistling stopped.

In the silence that ensued, the enormity of the love in Meredith's heart made her head swim all over again. "I'm afraid I need to lie down."

Three people were suddenly pulling her to her feet. Helping. Getting in the way. Rand swung his mother into his arms. "Emily, get the door. Martha, which way to her room?"

"Rand, put me down this instant, do you hear me?"

Everybody stopped in their tracks. Meredith smiled through her tears. "I mean it, young man."

Rand did as his mother instructed.

"Martha," Meredith said, her voice seeming to come from miles away in her own ears, "would you help me to my room? Emily, you can make the tea." She paused. "You never liked tea. Rand, you, either."

"Lie down, Mama," Emily said. "Rand and I will learn to like tea while you rest."

Meredith glanced behind her. Two of those faceless people she'd been dreaming about were no longer faceless. Her memory was still hazy, and she felt as if a light breeze might blow her off her feet, but she didn't want to close her eyes for fear that they would disappear. "You won't leave?"

Emily bit her lip and smiled through her tears as she shook her head. A sense of joy that Meredith had only dreamed existed flowed into her. So much didn't make sense, but now she needed to rest her body and her mind so she could take it all in.

"Come along," Martha said, taking Meredith's arm.

Moments before turning away and heading into the narrow hall that led to her bedroom, Meredith heard Rand say, "Just try to get rid of us, Mom. I dare you."

Shadows were long, the evening still, the sky the color of early twilight when Emily and Rand pulled out of their mother's driveway. "Please, God, I don't want to leave her," Emily whispered, tears running unchecked down her face as she waved.

"We have to, Em," Rand said, waving, too. "Dr. Wilkes is right. The longer we stayed, the more confused Mom became."

"Drive slow," Emily said around a sob. "I want to look at her as long as I can."

Their dear mother stood next to her therapist, waving for all she was worth. She looked dangerously pale, and achingly beautiful as she waved goodbye. In that last moment before they disappeared around a curve in the street, she blew them a kiss from the tips of her fingers.

Emily and Rand were quiet after that, each lost in similar thoughts. Their mother had slept for three solid hours, only to awaken with a screaming headache. No matter how much her head hurt, or how long she'd slept, she hadn't forgotten Rand and Emily. But she hadn't remembered any more, either. Emily didn't know who was more disappointed, her or them.

Dr. Wilkes had reminded them that, regardless of what she couldn't remember, she remembered them. It had been Dr. Wilkes who'd insisted they finally leave Meredith in her care. She and Rand had argued about that, but in the end, they'd admitted that she was probably right. This had been their mother's home for nearly ten years. It was Dr. Wilkes's belief that she would be better off in familiar surroundings, warning them that a sudden move at this point might cause a major setback. It was their mother, herself, who'd insisted Martha step up her therapy. She would try anything, she'd declared, including hypnosis again in order to regain the remainder of her memory, so she could go home, intact.

"Can you imagine how excited and thrilled everyone is going to be?" Emily exclaimed.

She and Rand had the same thought at the same time. "Not quite everyone," Rand said.

"The evil twin is going to be furious."

"My God, Em, when I think about everything she's done."

"I know."

"I wish it was safe for you to come back to D.C. with me."

They both agreed she would be safer in hiding back in Red River, Montana.

"I'm going to hate to leave Mississippi behind," she said. "Because it was here that I got to see you again. And Mom. Did I tell you I saw Amber, here, too?"

"Amber's in Mississippi? Are you sure?" Rand asked, in that infuriating way brothers had.

She gave him a look only sisters could manage, which pushed his buttons and made him defensive. "What would she be doing here?"

"I don't know. I thought maybe you knew. I haven't exactly been in contact with the family lately, remember? Amber must have a good reason. And something tells me it has something to do with the handsome, dark-haired man she was with."

"Amber is in Mississippi with a dark-haired man? This family is getting impossible to keep track of. And nearly impossible for me to keep safe."

"We're Coltons, Rand. We all have brains and good instincts. You men have brawn, and the women have feminine wiles. Something tells me Amber is using hers right now. Wherever she is."

Rand shuddered. He knew firsthand how it felt to be on the receiving end of an intelligent, determined woman's feminine wiles. Men were no match for that kind of strategy. If the youngest of his natural-born sisters was indeed using her feminine wiles right now, he felt sorry for the poor bloke she was with.

On the other hand, what a way to go.

Eight

The inn's door opened easily when Tripp nudged it with his elbow; Amber had left it ajar. The woman thought of everything.

As he shouldered his way through, he noticed that she appeared to be having a serious conversation with the no-nonsense woman standing near a desk in the next room. Apparently, there was a problem.

The bed-and-breakfast could have been lifted straight off the pages of a glossy magazine. It was Southern in style, with tall pillars and a verandah that stretched along the entire front. As long as it had running water and a couple of clean rooms, Tripp wouldn't have cared if it was a shack.

He looked around him in the foyer. This was no shack.

He'd paid the taxi driver, arranged his carry-on and most of Amber's bags over his shoulders and in his arms, then followed the course she'd taken up the wide brick walkway. He was hot and sweaty, his clothes wrinkled, his shirt stuck to his back. With every step, the thought of a cool shower and a quiet room grew more appealing.

"I have the confirmation right here." Amber lowered a shoulder bag to her feet and rifled through her purse.

Tripp stopped a few strides away. Whatever the problem, she seemed to be handling it. Which came as no surprise to him.

"According to this fax, dated two days ago," she said with quiet emphasis, "rooms ten and twelve are reserved in our names."

The other woman's countenance changed by degrees as she perused the fax. Next, she studied her register again. "Oh, dear."

Easing closer, Tripp said, "Problem?"

The other woman was probably fifty, and wore it well. Her auburn hair was smartly styled. Her diamond ring must have been three or four carats, her clothing as refined as the Southern lilt in her voice. "I don't know how it happened, but we just ushered two dentists and their wives from Iowa to rooms ten and twelve. They had confirmations, too."

The bags were getting heavy. "You're saying you don't have a room for us?" Tripp asked.

"Oh, no." She gave him a small smile. "We have a room for you."

Hoisting the bag that was slowly slipping from his grasp, he said, "Excellent. Where are they located? If you'd point us in the right direction, we'll find them ourselves."

He didn't know what to make of the furtive glance Amber and the other woman exchanged. It was Amber who answered. "Not them, Tripp. It. There's only one room reserved for us."

The innkeeper said, "If it's any consolation, I've always felt it was the loveliest room in the inn."

Tripp glanced down at Amber. Her hair was mussed, her lipstick long gone. She'd been traveling for hours. She'd been ill. How in the hell did she manage to look so damned appealing?

He needed some space.

He needed a shower, bad. And he needed both soon. "It doesn't matter if our rooms aren't next to each other," he said. In fact, it might be better if they weren't. Turning to the other woman, he said, "Put Amber in your loveliest room, and give me another one."

"I'm afraid everything else is taken, sir."

Amber knew the exact moment the full implication soaked through Tripp's sweat-glistened skull. It didn't take long. And he didn't look pleased.

She didn't know what to do or say. She'd verified these reservations herself. She'd considered every detail of this trip very carefully. By hook or by crook, she planned to woo Tripp into falling in love with her during the next forty-eight hours. Her last encounter with her mother had forced her to take a closer look at her reasons for remaining up north in the Fort Bragg area. Who would care if she left? She had friends everywhere. And really, if she put her mind to it, couldn't she do work for the Hopechest Foundation anywhere?

Meaningful work was important. Was being with someone who cared about her in return just as important? The answer was a whispered yes that started in her mind and ended in her heart.

Perhaps it was time for her to make a fresh start. Perhaps she would make one with Tripp. Some people believed they not only made their own fate, but they made the wave that carried them to it. Amber tended to be among those who believed a person could only control so much. She was all for catching a wave. She just didn't harbor any illusions, for sometimes, the perfect wave reared up and tossed a true believer on her rear.

She hadn't planned to fall in love with Tripp Calhoun. Now that she had, she wanted him to love her in return. She was going to give it her best shot.

She'd been thrilled to learn rooms ten and twelve had a connecting door, and positively ecstatic to discover that there had been a cancellation, and therefore they were both available. She'd shopped for hours for the perfect dress and shoes. She'd packed candles, her most beautiful dressing gown and her Enya CD. She'd planned the seduction of Tripp Calhoun right down to the tiniest detail. But even she hadn't had the audacity to be so obvious as to reserve only one room.

Apparently, providence was on her side. She hid a smile.

"Amber," Tripp said, "why don't you take this room? I'll get another somewhere nearby."

She hadn't planned that. She stared at him, speechless.

"Again, I apologize for the mix-up," the innkeeper said. "I would be happy to phone other inns and hotels in the area, but I'll be surprised if anything is available."

Amber didn't trust her voice, but the more the dear, kind, wonderful woman with the impeccable taste but only one vacant room talked, the more Amber liked her. "This is peak tourist season. To compound the problem, there are several conventions in this part of the city alone. The hotels are overbooked, and the local inns are already scrambling to accommodate everybody. I'll start phoning around. In the meantime, would you care to see the room?"

Amber watched with smug delight as Tripp shrugged.

"It is getting late," she said. "The rehearsal dinner begins at seven. It's going to take me a little while to freshen up and dress."

Finally, he nodded.

It would have been nice if he was a little more pleased about this new set of circumstances. But one thing at a time.

"RayAnn, would you come here, please?" the innkeeper intoned.

A younger version of the innkeeper suddenly appeared. "Yes, Mom?"

"Please help these people with their bags. And show them to room thirty, would you?"

RayAnn, a sturdy-looking girl of about sixteen or seventeen, snagged two of the bags Tripp had been holding. With a wink, she said, "If y'all would just follow me."

Talking as she went, the girl led the way through a large living room where a gray-haired, bespectacled man was looking askance at a woman wearing what could only be fake Spock ears, unless aliens really had landed in Mississippi. Still talking as if nothing was out of the ordinary, RayAnn led her little entourage up an open, Tara-styled staircase. At the top, she took a sharp right, and opened a hidden door. "Room thirty is the coolest room in the whole place."

The second flight of stairs was steep and narrow. RayAnn and Tripp were winded when they reached the small landing at the top. Amber had practically floated up them.

RayAnn was too busy unlocking the door to notice. Amber didn't look at Tripp to see if he had.

Stepping to one side to let them see, RayAnn said, "This is the only room on this floor."

Yes, Amber thought peering past the girl. Providence was most definitely on her side.

"What do you think?" RayAnn asked.

Amber and Tripp strolled over the threshold. The attic room was magnificent. It had a sloped ceiling and ankle-deep carpet the color of ripe plums. There was a quaint writing desk next to the door. Two overstuffed chairs on either side of an antique wardrobe were angled invitingly along the far wall. A king-size bed covered with a lux-urious duvet and a dozen textured and tasseled pillows dominated the room.

Staring at that bed, Amber drew a deep breath. This was where the heart of her plan would be carried out. If she dared.

Not if.

She dared.

She hoped.

Oh, for heaven's sake. Nearly every man she'd ever dated had been ready and willing to seduce her after the second date. But being the person actually doing the se-ducing was going to be a new experience. She should have taken notes.

Nerves fluttered up her spine. She forbade herself to tremble, and quickly looked away from the bed.

"You think this is something," RayAnn declared. "Wait'll y'all see the bathroom."

Amber glanced up in time to see Tripp, who'd been heading that way, freeze in his tracks, then swing blithely around as if he'd suddenly thought better of checking out the room.

"Don't tell me. Y'all are here for the dance conven-tion, right?"

Tripp's eyebrows lowered a fraction. "Dance conven-tion?"

"Well," the girl said, "you sure don't look like dentists or sci-fi fans."

Tripp continued to look puzzled. Amber smiled, because the sci-fi convention explained the fake Spock ears on the woman downstairs. "We're in town to attend a wedding."

While Tripp opened a door, revealing a television screen, RayAnn whispered, "You sure he isn't a dancer?"

"He's a pediatrician."

RayAnn pulled a face. "My pediatrician was about eighty."

Amber grinned. "So was mine."

"What do y'all think?" RayAnn asked loud enough for both of them to hear. "You want the room?"

"Would you give us a moment to discuss it?" Amber said.

With a wink, the robust girl backed from the room, drawing the door closed with her in the process. Alone with Tripp, Amber said, "I don't believe we have many options."

He stared at her, jaw set, teeth clenched. "You're willing to share a room with me?"

She looked at him for several seconds. His dark hair was disheveled, his light-blue cotton shirt wrinkled. His navy chinos rode low on his hips. He was lean and fit, and antsy as a caged cougar. It occurred to her that she wasn't the only one done in by all this traveling. She could tell he was trying not to take it out on her. It was one of the things she loved about him. She couldn't say that, however, at least not yet. So she said, "We lived in the same house one entire summer. I trust you." He had no idea how much, but he would before the night was through.

Tripp stared at Amber. He couldn't help it. Her hair was mussed, her face still pale with the aftereffects of her bout with airsickness. And yet her eyes were artful and serene, as inviting as cool shade on a sweltering day.

She trusted him.

Something was happening inside him. He was pretty sure no woman had ever entrusted her chastity to him. He felt at once humble and ten feet tall. And even more in need of that cold shower.

Damn.

He strode to the door, opened it and handed the girl the last bill in his pocket. "We'll take it."

He closed the door on RayAnn's smile.

"She's right," Amber said.

Tripp turned around. Amber was the one who'd taken the medicine, and yet he was the one who couldn't seem to put two thoughts together. "About what?"

"About you. You have the presence, the grace and the style, not to mention the moves of a dancer. Your name suits you."

"What does my name have to do with anything?"

"Tripp. It means to dance."

"You're kidding."

She lowered tiredly into one of the overstuffed chairs before looking up at him, a faraway light in her eyes. "You didn't know that?"

He shook his head. "My mother was a dancer before she had me."

"With the ballet?"

"Yeah, right." His lips twisted wryly. "In a club in L.A. That's where she met my old man."

She looked at him for what felt like a long time before saying, "We have something in common, you and I. We were both named after something our mothers loved."

Emotions stirred inside Tripp, heating him further. He didn't know what was happening to him. He was pretty sure he shouldn't be enjoying it so much, whatever it was.

His mother had died when he was seven. Other than an image of a woman with blond hair, a cigarette burning in an ashtray, a deep sultry laugh, and feeling safe when she was home, he couldn't remember much about that portion of his childhood. He'd had no idea his name meant to dance. She'd been a dancer. It seemed like too big a coincidence to be coincidental.

"Why don't you help yourself to the shower?" Amber said, rising slowly to her feet. "I'll unpack some of my things."

She bent over the bed and unzipped a case. He got a glimpse of beige lace and the upper swells of her plump breasts. After a long pause, during which he fought for self-control, he grabbed his carry-on and headed for the shower.

Tripp crossed his ankles and brought the medical journal closer to his face. Fascinating reading, medicine. There were never enough hours in a day to catch up on all of it.

He'd been staring at the same page for ten minutes.

Cool, calm and collected, he checked his watch, then started at the beginning of an article about a new AIDS medication for children, being developed by scientists in the south of France. He read the first line, and the second. Ah, yes, fascinating reading, medicine.

Fully dressed for the evening, he'd chosen a comfortable chair near the register where cool air was streaming into the room. His feet were propped on a matching ottoman. He had a comfortable place to read, an interesting topic to peruse. He found himself staring at the polished toe of his shoe.

The carpet was plush enough to absorb all but the faintest sounds. It was so quiet in the room he could hear the page crinkle as he brought the journal back into focus. Farther away, water bounced off tiles.

Amber was taking a shower.

He shook his head to clear it, checked his watch and read the second paragraph again. The words swam before his eyes, and instead of the medical procedure outlined in the article, he pictured Amber standing beneath the warm spray, the water gliding down her body.

He'd stood beneath the same shower half an hour ago. Only he hadn't used warm water.

A pipe rattled. In the next room the shower was turned off. He heard the thud of the shower door and absolutely refused to picture her drying her face, her neck, first one shoulder, then the other, and finally...

He scowled. Before the effects of his shower were completely undone, he grabbed the remote and pointed it at the TV. There. Some background noise was just what he needed. He should have thought of it sooner.

He read the paragraph a third time. And still had no idea what it said. Swearing under his breath, he jerked to his feet, strode to the door and gave it a brisk knock. "Amber, I'm going out for a—"

The door opened beneath his fist. Amber emerged wearing a creamy satin robe, her face scrubbed clean, her hair secured loosely on top of her head. Her eyes were luminous, her lips parted slightly as she said, "Yes, Tripp?"

A drop of water clung in the delicate hollow at the base of her neck. He cleared his throat. "I'm going out for a walk."

"Outside?"

He couldn't help it if his expression was snide.

"But it's ninety degrees outside."

His gaze did a slow slide down her body. Any second now, it was going to get hotter in here. Taking a step backward, he stripped off his tie and shrugged out of his suit jacket. "How long before you're ready?"

She glanced at the dress hanging in the alcove, and then at her reflection in the mirror across the room. "Forty-five minutes, give or take a few."

"I'll be back in forty-five minutes, give or take a few." He disappeared out the door without another word or a backward glance.

Alone in the room, Amber took in the blaring television and the medical journal tossed haphazardly onto the foot of the bed. Apparently, Tripp had had a difficult time concentrating. Poor baby.

The shower had been turned to cold when she'd gotten in. Evidently being in this close proximity to her was taking a toll on him. Poor, poor baby.

She turned off the television, hung his jacket over the chair then reached for her case. He would be back in three quarters of an hour, give or take a few minutes. She wanted to be ready when he returned. Girding herself with determination and courage, she peeled off her robe and got busy.

That poor baby hadn't seen anything yet.

Amber was standing in front of the full-length mirror, looking like something Tripp had only dreamed of when he walked through the door. He paused for a moment, taking in the sight of her. She looked up, her gaze meeting his in the mirror. Every hair on his body raised slightly, as if he was standing too close to an electric fence.

He'd never known another woman who could pull off wearing a dress that color. He didn't even know what to call it. Brown was too dark, beige too blah. The closest he could come to anything remotely like it was the outside of a walnut shell. And that seemed far too nondescript. So maybe it wasn't the color that made such an impression. Maybe it was the fit, the style, and the way, at first glance, it almost appeared as if she wasn't wearing anything at all. Every man on the planet knew how provocative almost could be.

"How was your walk?"

He shrugged one shoulder. "I only made it as far as the living room." He'd gotten caught up in a lengthy discussion about the health care system in Canada. He'd used the time to put up a new guard.

She was helping him in ways he would never be able to repay. She was his friend, dammit. Cooper was his friend. In her own way, so was Nurse Proctor. He had no trouble taking his eyes off either of them. Amber was a different story. Her dress was sleeveless, but not low-cut. It had an uneven hem, and was semitransparent from the knees, down. At first glance, the same appeared to be true of a three-inch band at her waist. It turned out to be an illusion. He knew, because he looked far longer than he should have.

His guard slipped a notch, and he had only himself to blame. Clearing his throat, he said, "I didn't really think you would be ready."

"I'm this close." She held up two fingers. That was when he noticed the tube of lipstick in her hand. She uncapped it and leaned closer to the mirror.

Mesmerized, he watched her outline her lips, then fill

them in with color. He gave himself a mental kick, grabbed his tie, and quickly tied it. Next, he reached for his jacket, reminding himself that it wasn't her fault he couldn't seem to keep his libido in check. She wasn't even looking at him. To her, this was just business as usual.

"I think I'm about set." She smoothed a hand down her sides. "I could use a little help with this zipper."

She reached up with one hand, lifting the few wavy tendrils of hair trailing down her neck out of the way. Tripp tried to keep contact at a minimum as he raised the zipper, but his fingertips still memorized the texture of her soft skin.

She swayed slightly, and in the mirror, he saw her eyelashes flutter. What was going on here?

Was this business as usual, or wasn't it?

He took a step back, watching her closely.

"Thanks." She said that one word in a voice soft and warm enough to slip into.

His guard slipped another notch. "Amber, what are you doing?"

She looked over her shoulder at him. "I'm getting ready. What does it look like I'm doing? All I need are my shoes." She slipped one on while she continued. "Are you ready to dazzle Montgomery Perkins and his associates, Doctor?"

Her voice sounded natural. Or did it? Before he could decide, she'd donned the other shoe and faced him.

"Well? How do I look?"

He thought she looked beautiful. He said, "You look tall."

She grinned. "It's these shoes. They cost as much as the dress did. They're to die for, aren't they? I mean, they make the outfit. Can I help it if, in them, I'll tower over that snotty little pipsqueak, Olivia?''

Tripp did a double take, then laughed out loud. The statement was just so Amber, he couldn't help it. The tension drained out of him. There was nothing new in the twinkle in her eyes. She wasn't up to anything. This was the same person he'd known when they were kids, the bratty girl with nerves of steel and a heart of gold. She'd grown up, but inside, she was the same little kid who'd stuck up for him to her father, only to call him a jerk the first chance she got.

He offered her his arm. ''Something tells me you're the one who'll be doing the dazzling tonight.''

Bag in hand, Amber placed her fingers in the crook of Tripp's arm. The most delicious sensation started in a place completely unconnected to her hand, only to radiate outward in every direction. She hoped he was right, and had to bite her lip to hold her expression to a demure smile.

Nine

Duncan's Restaurant in downtown Jackson wasn't quite as elegant as Alessandro's, but it was like Tripp had said when they'd first stepped out of the cab. Eating here was bound to be better than getting poked in the eye with a sharp stick. Amber had entered laughing.

This time it was she who didn't pay any attention to the heads that turned to look. She'd floated in on Tripp's arm, happy. She couldn't help it. She was thoroughly enjoying their weekend together. And she was more and more convinced that what they had would last.

Dr. and Mrs. Perkins had been warm and welcoming. And Amber had been genuinely taken with the bride-to-be and her groom. The bride's mother and all ten brides-maids had been friendly, too. Amber couldn't say the same for Olivia Babcock and Derek Spencer. Surprise, surprise.

Luckily for Amber, other than at dinner when she'd

sat across from Derek, she'd been exposed to him in small doses only. Olivia was more difficult to steer clear of.

Amber was standing with a small group of bridesmaids when Olivia, wearing a designer dress in royal blue silk, placed a dainty hand on Amber's arm and coyly said, "Those pins in your hair are tipped in amber, aren't they?"

Amber's nod was careful.

Olivia smiled all around as she said, "Amber on amber. How quaint and sweet. I had a similar fascination with sapphires when I was in junior high."

There was that poke in the eye with a sharp stick Tripp had mentioned. Amber swore everyone took a collective gasp. The bridesmaid on her right cleared her throat awkwardly, but Amber kept her smile pasted on her face and held her tongue, when what she wanted to do was wipe that smirk off Olivia's snotty face.

As unobtrusively and discreetly as possible, she excused herself from the little group the first chance she got, joining both mothers and the bride-to-be. Jennifer was fretting about the flower girl, who had refused to walk down the aisle at rehearsal. Her mother and Cornelia were trying to put her mind at ease.

Weddings. They involved so much hoopla.

Amber had been dreaming of hers forever. A long time ago she'd imagined an all-day, no-expenses-barred extravaganza such as tomorrow was sure to be. Not anymore. Fairy-tale weddings were for people with functional families. She couldn't imagine the stranger she called "Mother" helping Amber plan the wedding of her dreams.

She took a sip of champagne. Listening with only one ear to the wedding plans for tomorrow, she searched the semiprivate alcove for Tripp. It took only an instant to pick him out of the crowd. Fifteen minutes ago, Montgomery Perkins had escorted Tripp and his contender to the center of the room where they were deep in conversation with Dr. Gentry, Dr. Harris, and Perkins's older son, who happened to be an attorney practicing in Boston.

She was proud of Tripp tonight. This wasn't his preferred setting, and yet he'd handled himself with quiet dignity. At first glance he fit right in, in his expensive black suit and Italian tie. Sure, his haircut helped, but it only took a second glance to know there was something special about Dr. Tripp Calhoun. There was a natural, unaffected aura about him. It was there in the way he stood, his feet a comfortable distance apart, his shoulders squared, his head tilted slightly as he listened to something Dr. Gentry said. Tripp wasn't prone to smiles. When he grinned, he meant it.

In comparison, Derek Spencer smiled big and he smiled often. His hair looked a little too blond, his skin a little too tan. Surely, Amber wasn't the only person who thought Spencer's phoniness went deeper than his appearance. She simply couldn't imagine Dr. Perkins awarding the position to such a man.

Tripp chose that moment to glance her way. She couldn't see the color of his eyes from here, but she could feel the affection in his gaze. An answering heat found its way inside her, reminding her of everything she was planning for later in the evening. Nerves scrambled up and down her spine, but not enough to chase the hazy images out of her mind.

"Jennifer. Hello again."

Amber started, her attention coming back to the group

of women she was with. By the time she recognized that voice it was too late to retreat. Olivia was back.

"I was hoping I would get the chance to wish you the best for tomorrow. You must be so excited!" the petite brunette exclaimed.

"I was excited a year ago. A week ago. Tonight I'm nervous," Jennifer said.

"It's going to be lovely," Cornelia insisted.

"I hope it doesn't rain!" Jennifer's mother qualified.

"That's always a concern with a garden wedding," Olivia said, nodding in understanding. "But I heard a weather report. The weatherman is predicting sunny skies tomorrow and temperatures in the nineties. He's not calling for a drop of rain."

Jennifer Blakely was twenty-five years old, and undeniably pretty. Her relief seemed genuine as she laid her left hand on Olivia's arm. "Oh, thank heavens. I feel so much better!"

"If you girls will excuse us," Jennifer's mother said, drawing Cornelia with her.

Try as she might, Amber couldn't think of a graceful way to follow them. She was stuck, on guard, waiting for something bad to happen.

Olivia peered at Jennifer's hand. Lifting it into her own, she said, "What a gorgeous ring. Is that four carats?"

The other young woman shook her head sheepishly. "Five. David really shouldn't have, I know."

"But aren't you glad he did?" Olivia asked.

The two women laughed as if they were old friends. Turning to Amber, Olivia said, "I understand you and Tripp haven't set a date yet."

Keeping her voice carefully controlled, her expression schooled, Amber said, "No, we haven't."

"Your engagement came about rather suddenly, didn't it?"

Amber was trying to decide how to respond when Jennifer said, "A whirlwind romance? How romantic."

Amber could have hugged her.

"I couldn't help noticing that you're not wearing an engagement ring," Olivia said. "You really should insist on one. Without it, the engagement seems so, what's the word? Arranged, don't you think?"

Amber squeezed her wineglass so hard it was a miracle the stem didn't snap in her hand. She was so busy seething, she didn't notice the group of doctors slowly making their way toward her.

Jennifer didn't seem to notice, either. "What do you mean by arranged?" she asked.

Tamping down a nervous shudder, Amber said, "I believe Olivia has a flair for the dramatic. Arranged marriages went out of vogue a few hundred years ago. And as for rings..." Amber waved a hand in front of her face, sweeping the notion aside. "Don't get me wrong. I think diamonds are lovely." She paused for quiet emphasis. "My father owns shares in a diamond mining operation. Therefore, they're not as special to me as they are to some people. Besides, Tripp has something I find far more interesting and intriguing than any diamond. You know what I mean, don't you, Olivia?"

A few feet away, Tripp nearly choked on his champagne. Before his eyes, Olivia's expression changed. Her eyes narrowed and her lips thinned, as if she'd underestimated Amber and was only now realizing it. Any second now, a cat fight was going to break out.

Placing his glass on a passing waiter's tray, Tripp swooped between Amber and Olivia. "Dance?"

Amber didn't readily reply. Prying her glass from her

fingers, he placed it on the tray next to his, then led her to a corner where a three-piece orchestra was playing. "You and Olivia having fun?"

"That woman is evil. I don't know what you ever saw in her."

"Now there's a question." He turned her into his arms.

"I mean, how on earth could someone like you have had a relationship with someone like her? Even more mind-boggling is how she could toss you aside for someone like Derek Spencer."

Nudging her into a slow dance, he said, "First of all, it hardly lasted long enough to qualify as a relationship. And I'm the one who ended it."

"You did?" He could feel the smile vibrating through her. "Of course you did."

He spread his hand wide at her back, drawing her closer.

"I don't think your former fiancée likes me. Can you imagine that?"

Her wry humor worked over him like moonlight. Tripp almost smiled. He glanced across the room where Olivia was talking to Derek, their heads bent close. "You put her in her place. In her place isn't where Olivia Babcock likes to be."

"Thanks for the recap."

"Any time. You realize she's going to have to get even."

Even as she missed a step, and her mouth dropped open, something went warm inside him.

"Do you think it could hurt your chances with the medical practice?"

"Perkins just told me he's impressed with my work ethic."

She relaxed by degrees. "He's no fool."

Tripp was becoming accustomed to the zing that went through him every time he and Amber were together, but he wasn't accustomed to such ready praise. It went straight to his head. He drew her closer, letting the music set the pace, letting the burn deep inside him set the mood.

He hadn't expected to enjoy himself tonight. He would have been a lot more comfortable if he could lose his jacket, loosen his tie and roll up his sleeves. All things considered, the evening had been much more pleasant than he'd anticipated. It had a lot to do with the stimulating conversations he'd had with Montgomery Perkins and his sons. Not all rich people were shallow or superficial. Oh, all three of the Perkins men were blue bloods through and through. And all three dropped names of influential colleagues and their prestigious alma maters as if they expected Tripp to be impressed. He was a hell of a lot more impressed by how much they cared. About their chosen professions. About other people and about each other.

There was more to his enjoyment of the evening than stimulating conversations. It had to do with Amber. It was strange. His brain insisted nothing had changed between them, but his body begged to differ. He kept thinking about that damn room they were sharing. Room, hell. He kept thinking about that bed. Every time it happened, a change came over him, altering the rhythm of his heart, heating his blood, sending it chugging, thick and slow, to a part of him that was becoming increasingly difficult to ignore.

He was almost convinced it was all in his mind. Almost. But then she would look at him from across the table or across the room, and he didn't know what to think.

As the orchestra moved into another song, Tripp and Amber moved with it. Out of the blue, he dipped her, and she yelped in surprise. All around them, people turned to look. On her feet once again, Amber laughed.

Tripp couldn't take his eyes off her mouth.

She whispered, "I think Cornelia and Montgomery are pleased with the amorous attention one of their candidates is paying to his fiancée."

"Pretend fiancée, you mean."

She reached up with one hand, laying a finger against a vein pulsing in his neck. "Know what I think?"

He waited.

"I think that not all of it is pretend. And I think you know that as well as I."

A dozen denials raced through Tripp's mind, but only one sensation took hold deep in his body. He'd been aware of her curves tucked up close to his body the way all men were aware of all women in such close proximity. His body wasn't reacting to just any woman. All evening long he'd felt the undercurrent in the air. He'd lost track of how many times he'd reminded himself that he and Amber were friends. Just friends. All evening long he'd told himself it was just a simple case of loneliness, of sleeping alone for too long. He'd busied himself with the reason they'd flown to Mississippi, and he'd done his best to ignore the attraction.

Maybe he'd had too much champagne. Or maybe there was another explanation for the desire pouring through him. He drew far enough away to look into Amber's eyes.

"Be careful what you offer, Amber."

Her eyes were large and green and a hell of a lot more seductive than a friend's had any business being. "I know what I'm doing, Tripp."

The orchestra music faded into the background. His feet froze to the floor. All around him, couples danced on. He stood with Amber in the center of the dance floor, trying to resist her, all the while drawing her closer.

She looked at him, as if she knew exactly what he was thinking. As if a need had been building in her all day, too. As if she knew there was only one way to satisfy it.

"Jennifer and David are leaving," she whispered. "That means we can, too." She stepped out of his arms. "Shall we?"

They said their goodbyes to Montgomery and Cornelia, Jennifer and David, and half a dozen other people they'd just met. Walking toward the exit, Amber tucked her hand in the crook of Tripp's arm. "Making a grand exit is just as important as making a grand entrance."

They walked beneath an arch strung with white lights. Outside, Tripp placed a steadying hand on the ornate wrought-iron railing as he descended the steps. Amber smiled up at him as if she knew he could use all the steadying help he could get.

They were halfway down the steps when someone called his name behind them. He swung around. In the process, his knuckle caught on a rough spot on the railing. Tripp felt a slight pain in his hand. He was more concerned about the pain in the neck slanting him a phony smile.

"What do you want, Spencer?"

Derek Spencer made a show of looking Amber up and down before turning his attention back to Tripp. "May the best man win." With a snide curl of his lip and laughter that might as well have been canned, he turned on his heel and disappeared inside.

"What was that all about?" Amber asked.

"God only knows." Swiping a hand across his mouth, Tripp scowled.

Amber reached up and with gentle fingers took his hand in hers. Slowly, she brought it to her mouth and placed a kiss as soft as a whisper on his scuffed knuckle.

"When I was small, my mother used to kiss my scrapes and bruises to make them better."

She planted an openmouthed kiss on the next knuckle, and the next. "Better?"

His blood heated, thickened and slowly made its way south. He had a feeling that somewhere in the deepest recesses of her mind, she knew exactly what she was doing. She wasn't an innocent and she wasn't a child. She was a woman, a willing woman. One who was damned close to stepping over the line between lover and friend.

He was trying to remember all his reasons to hold her at arm's length when a taxi pulled up to the curb. Amber strode toward it. One hand on the door handle, she turned, waiting. She looked very sure of herself, and very determined.

She wasn't going to be easy to resist.

"It should be a lovely wedding. Jennifer is so nervous. Her little flower girl is only three. That's one of those iffy ages. You just never know what a three-year-old will do."

Amber had paused. It was the first breather she'd taken since leaving Duncan's Restaurant. Tripp glanced in the direction she was looking. The bed-and-breakfast was up ahead.

"Jennifer was afraid little Breanna would be too shy to walk down the aisle tomorrow." The silence hadn't lasted long. Amber opened the taxi door and climbed out.

He had little choice but to follow. "It turns out she just doesn't want to drop the pretty rose petals. She wants to keep them. Isn't that the sweetest thing you've ever heard? Did I tell you the bridesmaids are wearing lavender? Evidently, it's the most popular wedding color right now. Although black is big, too."

Tripp dug into his pocket for the fare.

The driver glanced from Tripp to Amber, who was still talking. And talking. When he next looked at Tripp, his expression was supportive. "Thanks, buddy. Your woman always this chatty?"

Tripp considered telling the driver that she wasn't *his* woman. And she wasn't normally chatty. He ended up shrugging and closing the door without saying a word.

Amber started toward the front door before the cab had pulled away. It was as if she was in a hurry. Tripp dragged his feet, ending up at the top of the second landing while she was taking the key from her purse and unlocking the door to their room.

Striding through, she said, "I can't wait to get out of these heels."

Before he could say one-Mississippi, she stepped out of one shoe. "Hold it right there."

She turned around as she leaned down to remove the other, as winsome and agile as a willow switch. "Are you going to close the door? Or shall I?"

He shut the door, then leaned against it. "What are you doing?"

"Whatever do you mean?"

As far as he was concerned, she could cut the innocent act. He was on to her. "You're chattering. And that isn't like you. Which means you're nervous. And if you're nervous, what the hell are you doing?"

"There's a fine line between being nervous and being

excited. And as far as what I'm doing, if you have to ask, I'm obviously not doing it very well."

The knowing glint that came and went in her eyes was a turn-on if he'd ever seen one. It made him uncomfortable as hell. And intrigued.

Damn. That ticked him off.

"You're trying to pick a fight." She looked him in the eye. "Maybe I'm doing something right, after all."

He felt his eyes narrow, a furrow form between his eyebrows. She should have been put off by his glare. For crying out loud, she should have been afraid.

"You're angry."

"Damn right I'm angry."

She was standing on the far side of the room, seemingly completely at ease. Reaching up with both hands, she began removing the amber-tipped pins from her hair. One by one, they dropped to the plush carpet without making a sound.

Tripp swallowed. "You should be afraid. Hell, at the very least you should be worried."

Holding his gaze, she removed the clasp that had secured the majority of her hair.

"But no. This is Amber Colton I'm dealing with. Everything comes naturally to you. You're not afraid of anything."

She shook her head, her hair falling around her shoulders in waves. "I'm afraid of some things."

"Like hell you are."

"I am." She took a tentative step closer.

"Name one."

"I'm afraid of spiders." Another several steps brought her far too close for his peace of mind. "I'm afraid of flying. I don't like elevators. Or gas stoves." Her voice was barely more than a whisper. "I'm afraid of wild dogs and terrorists, poisonous snakes, and drunk drivers, and deep inside, I am afraid of you.''

"Me?"

She nodded, taking another step closer. "I'm afraid you'll turn away from what I want tonight."

His ragged breath could have been heard anywhere in the room. "You're running out of time, Amber."

Another step brought her within inches of him. "What am I running out of time for?"

"Out of time to come to your senses."

She tilted her head understandingly, and Tripp realized he was the one running out. Out of breath, out of diversions, out of topics to argue about.

"Out of time to tell me no."

"That's an interesting way to put it, when I was just thinking how glad I am that we have all night."

The air rushed out of him in an audible whoosh. While he still had a few functioning brain cells, he said, "I didn't plan this. I didn't bring protection."

"I did."

He closed his eyes. When he opened them, there she was, just a touch away. "You planned this?"

"I brought candles, too. And romantic music."

His gaze homed in on her mouth. "You planned this."

"I don't think we need music or candlelight, do you?"

She swayed slightly. His hands shot out, perhaps to steady her, or perhaps to hold her safely away. Instead, he gathered her closer, his hands drawing her up, up.

She watched him through half-closed eyes and tilted her head. A moment later he covered her lips with his. The kiss was just a brush of air at first, but then it changed. Her eyes fluttered closed, as did his. He moved his mouth a quarter of an inch, deepening the kiss. He tasted champagne, and passion. Her lips parted beneath his, and a rush of feeling flooded over him. He made a sound deep in his throat, the kiss becoming a mating of lips, and tongues and the very air they breathed.

Tripp had always had a good imagination; heaven knew it had been working overtime tonight. But imagery couldn't hold a candle to the jolt pulsing through him right now. She was right. They didn't need candlelight or music. But they did need this.

They needed more.

Her body was fluid against his. Her waist fit his hands, the flare of her hips enticing him to explore. The kiss went on and on, their breath mingled, their sighs filling the room.

They finally drew apart, and their eyes finally opened. His hands went to her face. Holding her steady, he kissed her again, twice. This close, he heard her breath hitch in her throat. She took a step backward. For a moment he thought she'd come to her senses. It would be best. He didn't realize he'd been holding his breath until after she leaned down and switched off the overhead light, until after it became apparent that she hadn't changed her mind.

The only sound was his deep, shuddering sigh. The only illumination came from the table lamp across the room. It penetrated the darkness and threw soft shadows in every corner, on every hollow surface. The overhead fan moved the air in circular currents. It was romantic as hell. Dammit, he hadn't planned this, but somewhere deep inside him, he'd known the evening would end this way.

She'd thought of everything, even protection. He'd known she was thorough. He hadn't known she would be so pliant in his hands, or that he would want her so bad.

Without a word, she turned around. Reaching up with one hand, she moved her hair aside, presenting him with a silent request.

Hours ago he'd raised that same zipper. Now he bent down and planted a kiss at her nape. She shuddered beneath his lips. Inch by inch, he lowered the zipper to the small of her back. He knew what she wanted. Who was he to deny the lady?

Amber had never felt such a delicious sensation wash over her. Goose bumps skittered up and down her arms. Hesitating a moment, she took a silent breath for courage and gave in to the sheer pleasure of his touch. With a gentle hand on each shoulder, he turned her to face him. She forced her eyes open, and there he was, his smile stark and white and full of shared secrets, and of need.

She planted a kiss on his chin, then made short work of unknotting his tie. Next, she unbuttoned every button on his crisp white shirt. Her fingertips paused at his belt.

"You touch me there, and there'll be no turning back."

His eyes were so deep, so brown, so fluid, she felt herself slipping right in. Holding his gaze, she placed her hand where he'd warned her not to. His eyes closed, his breathing hitched. She'd never been so brazen, so wanton, had never felt so powerful. It was a heady sensation, but it was nothing compared to the expression on his face.

His eyes opened, his lips parted and then he dragged her against him as if he couldn't get enough, his hands memorizing every curve from hip to shoulder. Lowering her zipper the rest of the way, he eased the dress down her arms.

Forbidding herself to tremble, she let the dress slide

down her body. Ever so slowly, she stepped out of it and
kicked it aside.

She'd spent as much time finding the perfect lingerie
as she had searching for the dress and shoes. Standing
before Tripp in her transparent bra, the scrap of satin
panties and lace-topped stockings, she knew it had been
worth it. He couldn't take his eyes off the upper swells
of her breasts.

"Perhaps you would like to take it from here?"

Tripp didn't need a second invitation. He slid a strap
down each shoulder. She drew her shoulders together,
and for a moment, he thought she might cover herself
shyly. Something clicked far back in his mind. Before he
could examine it, she reached behind her, undoing the
clasp. In a luxuriant movement, she let the garment fall
to the floor.

He spread his fingers wide and covered her breasts.
Her body fit his so perfectly, he wanted to roll her underneath him. He tore off his tie and shucked his shirt.
His shoes came next. When he was naked, he whisked
her remaining wisps of clothing out of his way. Her eyes
had drifted closed, the look of rapture on her face his
complete undoing. He lowered her to the bed, stretching
out beside her.

The mattress shifted beneath their weight. He glided a
hand down her body, willing himself to slow down.

She whimpered. "Oh, don't stop."

"I'm not stopping, I'm just—"

She moved her leg against his. "I want—"

He knew what she wanted. He reached for protection.

He kissed her again, on the mouth, on her chin, her
shoulder, the delicate skin at her waist and hip. In that
order, and in every order.

"Ah, yes," she whispered. "Please."

He brought her on top of him, then in a movement that took both their breaths away he had her on her back and he entered her. She arched upward.

He was aware of something unusual. But then she started to move, and he couldn't think. It had been so long, and she was so beautiful, and sensual, and responsive. He tried to slow down, but she cried out, raking her fingernails down his back, letting him know she wanted nothing to do with going slow. Relying on instinct and the sounds Amber made deep in her throat, he gave in to need and followed her to that place beyond logic or reason, to that place that might as well have been on the other side of the moon.

He surfaced slowly. Once his breathing returned to a more normal rate, and he could actually think, he chastised himself.

It hadn't been a profound performance. Such things took time. And she hadn't given him any time, not to think, not to analyze, not to take things slow.

Sure as hell not to put two and two together and get four.

No wonder she'd been chatty. She'd said there was a fine line between nerves and excitement. Hell and damnation, she *had* been nervous—and for good reason.

Raising up on one elbow, he waited for her to open her eyes. "Amber, how…why?"

"Why, what?"

"Why didn't you tell me you were a virgin?"

She shrugged, bravely meeting his eyes. "I wasn't sure."

"You weren't sure."

Amber felt that, under the circumstances, it was only fair to forgive him for using that tone of voice. "I've wondered. I mean, I've had boyfriends, and once or twice

I thought…maybe…'' She ducked her head. "Guess not."

He moved to his side. "You guess not?"

She hid a smile. It was so like Tripp to get angry at a time like this. Honestly, she felt glorious.

"You guess not!" he repeated.

"Now I'm sure."

His mouth dropped open. "You're a beautiful woman, and you've undoubtedly had countless opportunities. Yet you never…until tonight. With me."

She averted her gaze, suddenly feeling shy, weepy and giggly and teary-eyed all over again. She needed a moment to herself to restore her emotions and preserve her dignity. First she said, "I was saving it for someone special."

He opened his mouth to argue, but she shook her head, silencing him.

"When I look back on this, I want to remember it as infinitely precious. I didn't want it to be with some guy after my family's money." She scooted to one side of the bed. "I'll be right back."

Just before closing the bathroom door, she glanced over her shoulder. The sight of him, so masculine and virile, sexually spent, at once baffled and thoroughly ticked off, brought a smile to her lips. A look of shock crossed his face. And then, as if he couldn't help himself, he smiled at her in return.

"You okay?" Tripp asked when Amber returned from the bathroom ten minutes later.

Her smile was radiant, making her nod unnecessary. Sitting down on the edge of the bed, she glanced at him, then quickly, shyly away. "Maybe I should ask you that question."

Tripp stopped fiddling with his watch. She was wearing her cream-colored dressing gown. She hadn't taken it in with her, which meant she'd thought ahead and had planned that, too. Curious, he asked, "Was there really a mix-up in the room reservations, Amber? Or was that your doing, too?"

She lifted the blankets and climbed into bed. It might have been an awkward moment, and yet she didn't appear uncomfortable. When she was settled on the pillows, she turned her head and looked at him, her eyes large and green and clear. "I was hoping for this." With a sweep of her hand, she gestured to the bed, and what had gone on a short time before. "I really had requested rooms ten and twelve because they had a connecting door. This attic room," she said, with another sweep of her hand, "must have been the work of divine intervention." She gave him a moment to digest the information, then asked, "Do you believe me?"

He stared at her long and hard. When he nodded, something ignited inside Amber, something far deeper than her skin. Love swelled in her chest. She longed to hear him say he loved her in return. Knowing he believed her was almost as precious.

He must have switched the table lamp off and the light on his side of the bed on while she'd been freshening up. He was propped up on pillows, half in the shadow of her bedside lamp, the sheet and duvet pulled up to his waist. She turned onto her side, facing him, tucking the sheet under her arms.

"Now," he said in a tone of voice men used when they wanted answers, and they wanted them now. "Why don't you tell me how a woman as smart and beautiful as you, a woman who's had three *real* marriage proposals could have gone this long without making love."

She'd been expecting the question, and yet she still wasn't sure how to explain. She owed it to him to try. "Let's just say that if the proposals were accompanied by love, it was for my family's money."

"Did you love any of them?"

"I liked them. One in particular. But in the end, it was all about what my father's money could buy for him. Cars, boats, gifts, vacations."

"Positions in medical practices?"

She shook her head earnestly. "This is different. You don't even want that position. You're only doing it to help the poor. Believe me, the only poor my last boyfriend wanted to help was himself. He wanted a trip to Paris. My participation was optional. Believe me, you're the only man who's ever wanted more from me than my father's money."

"Poor little rich girl."

"I don't want your pity."

"You're too smart and conniving and headstrong for me to pity."

She grinned. A lot of people had told her she was beautiful. Perhaps some of them had even meant it. But no one's praise had ever meant more to her. She loved him. Lord, she was happy. "Tripp?"

"Hmm?"

"I don't really feel like talking anymore."

His hair was tousled, his face lean and chiseled. There were shadows beneath his eyes, an appreciative glint in them. His chin was just beginning to bear the evidence of a beard. His shoulders were broad, his chest muscled, the hair sparse. He started to move, as if to turn out her light. She reached up with one hand, halting him.

"I don't really feel like sleeping, yet, either."

He lowered his arm as if in slow motion. "You don't."

SANDRA STEFFEN					175

It wasn't a question. She shook her head ever so slightly anyway. "Until tonight, I never knew real passion, how it felt, how it sounded, tasted. I brought more than one, um, er, package of protection."

"How many more?"

"The whole box."

His gaze left her face, trailing to her neck and shoulders, and finally back to her eyes. "That's a tall order."

She went up on one elbow. "Then you're up for the challenge?"

He rolled her underneath him without warning. "What do you think?"

"I think..." Her voice trailed away on a sigh. "Oh, my..."

The mattress creaked beneath their shifting weight. His hand slipped between their bodies. He covered her breast with his palm, and her lips with his.

"This time," he said when the kiss ended, "we're going to do this my way. Nice and slow."

She made an acquiescent sound in the back of her throat.

He slid his hand along her neck, and slowly down all the way to her navel. Her breath hitched in her throat as she said, "Whatever you say, Doctor. Whatever you say."

"That's more like it."

He repeated the caress. And the time for talking came to an end once again.

Ten

"**D**early beloved, we are gathered here today to join Jennifer and David in holy matrimony..."

Still winded, Amber and Tripp breathed a sigh of relief. They'd made it. Barely. They'd slipped into their seats next to two women wearing big hats mere seconds before the first bridesmaid started down the makeshift aisle. The breeze meandered across the expansive lawns, ruffling the dog-eared pages of the reverend's prayer book. That same breeze fluttered the hems of the bridesmaids' satin dresses, gently billowing through all the yards of delicate tooling that comprised the bride's breathtakingly elegant veil.

Amber sighed. The setting was beautiful and timeless, the stuff fairy tales were made of. The large, sweeping lawns were immaculately groomed. Even the hundred-year-old oaks were dressed for the occasion, their moss-laden branches spread wide and proud. Magnolia and wisteria, pink and white roses, dogwoods, azaleas and black-eyed Susans bowed in the wind, lending their natural beauty to the joyous occasion. The sky overhead was sunny. It seemed that even the gray clouds in the west were standing at attention far away from the garden wedding.

"Do you, David James Perkins, take this woman to be your lawfully wedded..."

Songbirds twittered. Harp music wafted softly in the background.

"...to love and to cherish..."

Amber smoothed her hands over the goose bumps on her arms. It might be eighty-eight degrees in the shade, but Amber always shivered at weddings.

She loved weddings. All her life she'd dreamed of hers. Now she was certain there was only one man in all the world she wanted as her groom. Oh, she wished— She didn't allow herself to finish the thought. Wishes like that were risky. She knew it was too soon but she also knew she was completely in love with the man sitting next to her.

Tripp wasn't exactly averse to her, either. Oh, he hadn't said it in so many words, but she'd always been a firm believer that actions spoke louder than words anyway. And Tripp had proven to be a man of inventive and breathtaking action.

The breeze picked up, fluttering the streamers on the end of every row, lifting the collar of her silk suit, blowing her hair across her face. She tucked the loose strands behind her ear, then crossed her legs, the action drawing her attention to a slight tenderness that called to mind the most delightful activities.

She'd studied her face in the mirror earlier, wondering if she looked any different today. Luckily, her sage-green suit covered the whisker burn on her shoulder. Surely, nothing could conceal the dewy look in her eyes. She didn't want to conceal it. She wanted to whisper her love for Tripp, shout it, write it in the sky.

Glancing up at him, she wondered if men bore any physical evidence of such things, or if they simply forgot about making love as soon as it was over. She tugged the hem of her skirt down, and noticed that his gaze followed the movement. Looking closer at him, she saw a vein pulsing in his neck. As far as clues went, it was very telling. She hid a smile.

The area surrounding her heart grew warm, and it had nothing to do with the heat and humidity. She combed her fingers through the hair being mussed by the wind, then, trying not to fidget, folded her hands in her lap.

She hadn't planned to wear her hair down. Actually, she'd been in the process of putting it up when Tripp had walked up behind her with other ideas. She had no other frame of reference, but surely other men didn't have his stamina.

She smiled to herself. His stamina had nearly made them late.

Organ music drew her from her musings. The ceremony was over and David was kissing his bride.

The ladies with the big hats drew Amber and Tripp into a conversation about Southern architectural restoration. Amber was doing most of the talking; therefore, she didn't pay much attention when Olivia Babcock walked past, alone.

Tripp noticed. He noticed Steven Gentry and Winston Harris conversing with Derek Spencer in hushed earnestness on the other side of the receiving line a few minutes later, too. Tripp was always on edge where Derek was concerned. He figured that if the Creator had

given the man scruples, Derek had offered them back—
for a fee, of course.

After making their way through the receiving line,
Tripp and Amber strolled toward a rose-laden arch mark-
ing the entrance to the area of the garden where the reception was to be held. They hadn't gotten far when
Steven Gentry and Winston Harris materialized out of a
small crowd.

"Dr. Calhoun."

Tripp's eyebrows lifted slightly. Today it was Dr. Calhoun; last night it had been Tripp. "Yes?"

Both older doctors squared off directly in front of him.
"On behalf of Montgomery and Cornelia, and Jennifer
and David, we feel...that is..." Gentry's voice trailed
away.

Tripp found himself standing up straighter, on red
alert. Amber must have sensed something, too, for she
went perfectly still at his side. "Yes?" he said again.

Harris took his turn. "Under the circumstances, we
feel it would be best if you left."

"Under what circumstances?"

A movement to the right drew Tripp's attention. For
the first time that day, he saw Derek Spencer in plain
view. His biggest adversary was as impeccably groomed
as always. The black eye, however, was brand-new.

"As we were saying," Steven Gentry said. "Under the
circumstances, it would be best if you left quietly."

Amber spoke for the first time. "Why would that be
best?"

Gentry and Harris shared a look.

Derek strode a little closer. "That's a hell of a right
hook you have, Calhoun. I thought you gave up fighting
after college."

"Exactly what are you implying?" Tripp asked, his voice carefully controlled.

Derek shook his head, and made a *tsk, tsk, tsk* sound.

"You told them that Tripp hit you?" Amber asked, her voice rising an octave.

In lieu of a reply, Derek gingerly patted his swollen eye.

"You lying sack of—"

"Please," Gentry said. "Save the street talk."

Derek spoke then. "Guess you can take the kid off the street, but you can't take the street out of the kid."

Tripp took an ominous step in Derek's direction. The other man took a hurried step back. As far as acts went, it looked very convincing. Sickeningly so.

Amber turned to Dr. Harris and Dr. Gentry, imploring them with her look. "I was with Tripp all evening. He didn't blacken Dr. Spencer's eye."

All three men made a point of staring at the scuffed knuckle on the hand Tripp had automatically made into a fist. Tripp glanced at his hand, too, and then at the man who had been like slivers under his fingernails, "You told Perkins I hit you?"

There was a boastful glint in Derek's eye when he said, "No. I told Montgomery I had a little run-in with a door after dark. Today is his son's wedding. I didn't see any point in spoiling it for him."

Tripp just bet. He could picture the scenario in his mind. And it was all beginning to make sense. Derek had witnessed Tripp scrape his hand on the railing when he and Amber had been leaving the restaurant last night. Spencer always did have a nose for opportunity.

Cramming his hands on his hips, Tripp said, "Rather than run to Montgomery with your story, you told his two associates."

"He came to us, yes," Steven Gentry said, anger in his voice.

Winston Harris said, "Derek insists he doesn't want to press charges. We disagree, but he says the two of you go back a long way, therefore he's willing to let bygones be bygones. We'll tell Montgomery you've had a change of heart. You'll want to put your regrets in a formal letter."

A thin chill hung in the air as Tripp looked at Spencer. "You know I didn't lay a finger on you."

Spencer said, "I understand that you have to say that. Come on, Tripp, what else are you going to say under the circumstances?"

Amber bristled at Tripp's side. Turning to Harris and Gentry, she said, "It's Tripp's word against Derek's."

Gentry shook his head. "If that were true, we wouldn't be having this conversation."

"What do you mean?"

"Derek had a witness," Harris said.

"Who?" Amber asked in a choked whisper.

Just when Tripp thought things couldn't get any worse, Olivia materialized out of nowhere. Taking a dainty step in his direction, she said, "May I have a word alone with you, Tripp?"

Tripp sensed Amber's reluctance to step aside, but she did so without a word. Olivia threaded her fingers through Tripp's, leading him to a shaded area several feet away, out of hearing range of everyone else.

"You know I didn't hit your boyfriend, Olivia."

"I know what really happened, yes."

"Then you'll—"

She touched her finger to his lips to quiet him. Placing her other hand on his arm, she squeezed provocatively.

She had a strong grip for someone with hands so small. She always had.

"That depends on you, darling."

A primitive warning sounded in Tripp's brain. He waited, staring at that perfect skin, those perfect teeth and nose and chin.

"Your hair looks incredible," she said, her voice a breathy whisper. "I liked it long, but this is even better. Now a woman has to look closer to see the warrior underneath."

Once, her smile had sneaked up on him, her open pursuit of him had been flattering. Today she left him cold.

"You have the opportunity to do the right thing, Olivia. Tell Gentry and Harris the truth."

"All right."

He drew his first easy breath in several minutes.

"On one condition."

That easy breath was choked off at the halfway point. "What condition?"

She pouted. "So much anger."

"What condition, Olivia?"

"I'll tell Steven and Winston what really happened." She paused, wetting her lips. "But there's something I want in return."

What Tripp saw in the eyes gazing up at him repulsed him. "What do you want?"

"I want another chance."

For the life of him, he couldn't understand how someone with everything could have so little. "Another chance at what?"

"Don't be obtuse. It doesn't become you. Do you really want me to spell it out for you?"

"You want another chance with me."

Her smile was victorious. "Yes."

"No."

Her face showed her surprise. Just like that, her eyes iced over and her smile disappeared. The flush that crept up her neck clashed with her periwinkle dress. "What do you mean, no?"

"If you don't understand the concept, look it up."

A brittle silence followed.

She took a sharp breath, and finally said, "You're making a mistake."

"I don't see it that way. If you knew me at all, you'd know I don't lie."

On the other side of the magnolia bushes, Amber placed her hand over her mouth to hold in all the murmurs and heartfelt sighs trying to slip out. The groom's grandfather had taken Spencer, Harris and Gentry to speak with someone elsewhere in the garden. Amber had seized the opportunity and slipped into the bushes. She wished there was something she could do to help Tripp, as she had when they were kids.

She'd known she was in love with him last week. Last night she'd fallen a little further and a lot deeper. Suddenly she understood why people said love had no bounds. She wanted to shout for joy, do a cartwheel, gloat.

Olivia was still talking. And Tripp seemed to be handling the situation on his own.

She remembered another time a week or so ago when he'd insisted he didn't lie. She was inordinately pleased that he didn't tell Olivia that lies were like dogs, seemingly harmless to your face, only to turn on you the instant you let down your guard. He saved the really good material for Amber. Was it any wonder she loved him?

"Don't expect me to believe your quickie engagement to that Colton wench is the real thing."

"Watch it, Olivia."

"What? Did I strike a nerve? I didn't think you were the type to lose your head over a pair of C cups."

It was a good thing Amber's hand was over her mouth. It was probably a good thing she wasn't closer, too. She would have been tempted to slap Olivia.

"Actually, you're right," Tripp said. "I'm more attracted to integrity and honor. You might want to look those up, too."

Amber was wiping a tear from her eye when Olivia stormed away. Before someone asked what she was doing in the magnolia bushes, she stepped out of them, brushing at the leaves clinging to her skirt. Deciding there was nothing she could do about the run in her stocking, she strolled around to the other side.

She and Tripp were alone in this portion of the garden. Eyeing the leaves sticking to her jacket and the twig tangled in her hair, he said, "You were eavesdropping again?"

If she'd had the time, she would have explained that she hadn't eavesdropped in years. Actually, she only seemed to listen in on conversations where Tripp was concerned. But she didn't have the time, so she simply nodded truthfully, and said, "What are you going to do?"

His shoulders were squared, his jaw set, his lips thinned with irritation. He looked past two old men who were staring at the sky, to the garden where the wedding reception was getting under way, and then in the opposite direction where a wide, sweeping flagstone path led to the front of the house. Through clenched teeth, he said, "I guess it's time to hail a cab."

Her mind whirled at his dry response. "If we leave, they win."

"They've already won."

"But—"

"Derek provided Gentry and Harris with exactly what they ultimately wanted. They'd made up their minds weeks ago. Not only do they have leverage, now they have the ammunition, too, along with the muscle to back up their narrow-minded decision."

"But—"

"If we stay, it'll only make a scene, and I'd rather not be responsible for ruining Jennifer and David's wedding." He started up the slope to the side of the sprawling antebellum house.

She absolutely refused to say "but" again. "There must be something we can do," she called, holding her ground.

He turned. "Do you want me to lower myself to Derek and Olivia's level?"

She shook her head slowly, because no position was worth that. She hated situations like these. But he was right. There was little that they could do that wouldn't involve ruining the day for Montgomery, as well as for David and Jennifer. Perhaps they could do something to cause Harris and Gentry to doubt Spencer's word. But there was nothing more they could do today.

Amber and Tripp reached the driveway in silence. They were striding past one expensive American-made and imported car after another when thunder rumbled. "Oh, no," Amber said, racing to a waiting taxicab. "What else could go wrong?"

The sky opened up, and it started to rain.

It was foggy and nearly dark by the time they passed the city-limit sign in Fort Bragg. At least it wasn't raining back home in California.

Since neither of the landing strips in Fort Bragg had towers or runways long enough for jets, Amber and Tripp had flown in and out of Mendocino. From there, it was only a ten-mile drive to Amber's house.

Tripp had been pensive throughout the trip from Mississippi. Unfortunately, Amber's medication had made her groggy, and no matter how hard she'd tried to stay awake, she'd slept most of the way home.

She stirred when he pulled into her driveway. Secretly, she was worried. Since it looked as if he wasn't going to be chosen for that position down in Santa Rosa, would he convince himself that there was no need to continue their relationship?

He'd opened his door, popped the trunk and had half of her bags in his hands when she joined him at the back of his car. Dragging a few cases into her own arms, she said, "Did you spend the entire trip home thinking about Spencer's victory?"

Tripp shrugged. Actually, he'd thought about money problems and bills and the high cost of medicine. And her. Damned if he knew what he was going to do about any of those things.

She maneuvered the key out of her purse without dropping anything. Once the door was opened, he followed her inside, then lowered the bags to the floor in her foyer. She glanced at him. He looked at her. It was strangely awkward. "I should be going."

Slowly, she placed the bags she'd carried in on the floor in the next room. "Are you sure you wouldn't like to stay awhile?"

"I wouldn't be good company. And I'm in no mood to talk."

"What I have in mind doesn't require talking."

SANDRA STEFFEN   187

His gaze settled on her mouth. His thoughts slowed, his body heated.

"Actually," she said, talking as she switched on a lamp in the living room. "I know of two activities that would take your mind off your troubles."

"Two?"

His voice had lowered. Her knowing smile didn't help in the least.

"Meditation." She plugged in a tabletop fountain and instantly water gurgled softly. With a press of a button, mood music surrounded them. "Meditation, and what you're thinking. I vote for the second activity, too."

The enchantress grinned.

His heart hammered away at a steady beat. "Anybody ever tell you you're a brat?"

"Only you."

He stared deep into her eyes, and was nearly lost all over again. He hadn't realized he'd left the foyer. Since she was still standing near the lamp she'd switched on, he must have been the one who had moved. In some far corner of his mind, he knew he should resist. He didn't want to resist. When she reached up on tiptoe and kissed him, he couldn't help himself. He kissed her back.

His arms wound around her back, molding her to him. He'd memorized every curve, every hollow, every inch of her body last night. Suddenly he had to discover her all over again.

He touched her through her clothing and she through his, but they couldn't get close enough. Their sighs and groans mingled with the sound of water gurgling over rocks in the tabletop fountain. Meadowlarks sang harmony to piano and a lone stringed instrument. It was supposed to be relaxing music. It did cover the quiet, but it sure as hell didn't quiet his sudden burning desire. He needed more. More closeness. More passion. More of everything she had.

He maneuvered her backward until her back was against the wall. Taking her face in his hands, he kissed her again, long and deep. All the while, his body pressed into hers. Closer. Closer.

Still not close enough.

She was the one who broke the kiss. She was the one who deftly unbuttoned his shirt. Next, she undid her own. Finally, they were skin to skin, chest to chest, man to woman. A shudder went through him. This still wasn't close enough.

"We can do this standing up," he said, his voice a low growl in his own ears. "Or you can take me to your bed. It's your choice."

She kissed him once more and then she stepped out of his arms and started toward a dark hallway. He followed her into her room, then stood and watched as she turned back the covers. "Is this what you had in mind?" she asked.

Her voice was like the wind after midnight, a deep sigh, a gentle mooning, a slow sweep across his senses. He was reaching for her again when a sound, like a small explosion, tore through the room.

He whirled around without thinking, placing himself between her and the window. He braced himself, his eyes wide, his breathing ragged.

His eyes were just beginning to focus again when it occurred to him that a car had backfired out on the street. This wasn't the streets in L.A. And he wasn't a kid living and fighting and sometimes nearly dying on them.

A bell jangled, and he jumped all over again. When it sounded again, he turned around and swore under his breath.

Amber was looking at the phone on her nightstand. That was what was ringing. Understanding dawned.

"The answering machine will get it," she whispered, pressing a kiss into his shoulder.

Tripp's heart slowed down, then sped up when the answering machine clicked on. "Amber, this is Rand. I need to talk to you. If you're there, pick up, would you?"

She went perfectly still, her indecision palpable. "Rand never calls me. Something must be wrong."

Since Tripp was closer to the phone, he scooped it up and handed it to her. The lingering smile she gave him as she placed the phone to her ear warmed him in ways that made it damned difficult to move.

"Rand, how are you?"

Tripp took a deep breath. Raking a hand through his hair, he walked to a bookcase on the far side of the room.

"Yes, I was in Mississippi. How did you…" She listened for a moment. "In Jackson, yes…but how…" Tripp felt her eyes on him as she murmured, "Mm-hmm. You remember Tripp Calhoun…"

There was another stretch of silence.

"How did you know? Rand, what's going on? You never call me. And what were you doing in Jackson?"

Amber glanced at Tripp. He was buttoning his shirt. She started toward him, then stopped, torn. "Rand, would you hold for a minute?"

She laid the phone down. "Tripp?" The expression on his face made her feel as if she was walking on eggshells. "Are you leaving?" she whispered.

He tucked his shirt in while he answered. "That call sounds important."

His gaze strayed to the skin exposed by her open shirt. She hoped that was a good sign. "You're right." She kept her voice quiet so her brother wouldn't hear. "Rand never calls unless it's important. But that doesn't mean you have to go.''

''It's been a long weekend.''

What pride she had left, she swallowed. ''I thought it was a wonderful weekend. What are you going to do now? About your clinic, I mean?''

''I don't know. I'll figure something out.''

Giving him a thorough once-over, she said, ''I'd like to see it.'' She held her breath.

''You would?''

''You could show me yours, and I could show you mine.''

Tripp felt sideswiped by her smile. ''Are we still talking about work?''

''If you say so.''

Her eyes were dark green tonight. He knew for a fact that they could flash with insolence one second, tease the next.

Tripp was a man who lived by a code that was dictated by ethics and gut instinct. Something was bothering the back of his mind. He didn't know what it was. He only knew he wouldn't be able to figure out what it was if he stayed here and finished what they'd started. He had to leave.

First, there was something he had to do.

He reached her in three long strides, grasped her by the shoulders and kissed her, swift and sure. Setting her away from him, he said, ''If you stop by the hospital after work tomorrow, I'll give you a guided tour of my clinic.''

''All right.'' She sounded breathless.

A brand-new rush of desire flooded into him. Fighting the impulse to say to hell with whatever was bothering the back of his mind, he nodded once and left her to her telephone call.

Amber took a deep breath. She didn't breathe again until after she heard her front door click shut. Picking up the phone, she said, "Yes, Rand. I'm still here."

An unwelcome tension had settled to her stomach and she realized just how precarious her ties to Tripp were. He wanted her, physically. He'd made that perfectly clear.

She listened to her brother, but all the while a tiny voice in her head insisted that there was more to Tripp's feelings for her than desire. She didn't know why he'd suddenly decided to leave. She wished he hadn't.

She was seeing him again tomorrow night. Hopefully, she would know more then. Who was it who said knowing was half the battle? Unfortunately, it wasn't always the most difficult half. Not when she was dealing with a man as complicated as Tripp.

"What? Of course I'm listening… Yes, I'm fine, really. Rand? Just how difficult did Lucy make things for you early in your relationship?"

Her big brother said something to the effect that it was hell, but most of that was his doing, not Lucy's, then asked about Sophie and River and little Meggie. Amber answered truthfully. "Sophie's fine. They're all fine. But what did you do to secure your relationship with— What? Drake? I haven't talked to him in a while, but I think he's all right… Liza and Jackson, too. We still haven't heard from Emily. And I'm worried."

He interrupted her again.

She flopped down on the bed. "Dad stays away a lot. And Mother, well, you know how she is…"

The fountain gurgled in the next room, and the mood music changed from a mountain meadow to an ocean's whisper. Now that Tripp had gone, it looked as if she was going to have to meditate to relax. First, she wanted to have a heart-to-heart talk with her oldest brother. Instead, it was twenty questions.

Why was it that guys were so willing to ask questions, and so unwilling to answer them?

She sighed. Men.

Eleven

"**I**'m the one who risked life and limb today, Calhoun. Why are you the one who's pacing?"

Tripp released all his breath before turning around, his back to the window. Coop was sitting in his usual chair, his feet propped on Tripp's desk in the usual way. He was right. Compared to Coop's day, Tripp's had been uneventful. Which only meant that his unease didn't stem from work. But he'd known that.

The small county hospital had been buzzing for hours with talk about the battered wife who'd stumbled into the E.R. only to collapse at Dr. Gavin Cooper's feet. Normally, Coop was pretty unflappable, but this one had gotten to him.

"You okay?" Tripp asked.

For once, Coop's grin wasn't very convincing. "I should be used to having women fall at my feet."

"I heard she filed a police report. She's pressing charges against her husband this time."

Several seconds passed before Coop answered. "He broke two of her ribs, dislocated her shoulder, bloodied her nose and blackened her eye. After that he stopped being nice."

Tripp remained quiet, letting his friend vent.

"She said she should have known it was coming. Hell, she was trying her damnedest to blame herself. He fits the wife-beater MO to a T. Rich or poor, they're all alike. He talked her into quitting her job when the kids started coming. Guys like that need a woman to be completely dependent on them. That way, when his temper blows, the little woman is a sitting duck, with no choice but to take it."

Coop's terminology raised the hair on the back of Tripp's neck. A sitting duck? That phrase was imbedded in the back of his mind. He couldn't place why.

"She has a choice now, Coop."

Gavin Cooper raked his fingers through his hair. "Guess you're right. She and her kids are hidden away at a shelter, safe for now. Maybe after the cops pick up the bastard, they'll stay that way."

"You did a good thing today."

Coop uncrossed his ankles and lowered his feet tiredly to the floor. Running a hand through his hair, he scowled. "Look at me. My brow's furrowed, my teeth are clenched, my jaw set. Fred just accused me of taking lessons from you."

"Be thankful he didn't accuse you of taking lessons from Proctor."

The ploy worked. Coop grinned for about a second. "I'm due at the clinic in ten minutes. Guess I'd better get out of here."

"I can take your shift at the clinic tonight."

"Nah. I'd rather keep busy. When I'm finished there, I think I'll call a leggy blonde, brunette or redhead. A good roll between the sheets would go a long way in relieving my stress."

A soft knock sounded at the door. Both men looked up, and there was Amber, a vision in cream and gold, her eyes wide, her smile tentative.

"Just what the doctor ordered," Coop said.

She eyed both men dubiously. "May I come in?"

Tripp said, "Enter at your own risk."

When Amber smiled, Tripp felt a tightening in his throat and a chugging in his chest. He was either having a heart attack or there was something worse wrong with him.

He took a deep breath and caught a whiff of the same exotic, flowery perfume she'd been wearing Saturday night. Forget Coop's mention of a leggy brunette or redhead. Tripp wanted another night of lovemaking with a certain blonde. But whatever had been bothering him last night was still bothering him today. He'd lost count of how many times a distant, out-of-focus memory had swirled into his brain. Every time he came close to bringing it in clearly, the memory of Amber, in the throes of a strong passion, heated his thoughts and turned his attention elsewhere.

It was happening now. Oh, no it wasn't. He gave himself a mental shake and forced his thoughts into a semblance of order. He saw Coop rise slowly to his feet.

Eyeing his scrubs, Amber said to Coop, "Nice outfit."

"If you ask real nice, I'll take 'em off. If you ask real nice, I'll take anything you want off."

"I don't know how women refuse such a sincere offer," she said on a smile. Then the grin faltered. "Is that blood on your shoe?"

He glanced down. "Don't worry, it isn't mine."

Amber stared deep into Coop's eyes. She knew his type. A player, and handsome in his own right, he had blue eyes, a grain of goodness and a lazy, seductive grin that had left a trail of broken hearts in its wake.

Her heart was taken, therefore, she was immune. "Bad day?"

"Forget about today. Why don't you ditch the Lone Ranger there and run away with me?"

She laughed in spite of herself. "Is that what they call him? The Lone Ranger? I hadn't heard that. But I have heard people call you the Don Juan of County General. Why do I get the feeling you aren't proposing marriage?"

"Hell, if a marriage proposal would do it, I could arrange one."

She nudged Coop with her shoulder and said drolly, "Do you always hit on your friend's dates?"

Amber wasn't at all comfortable with the surprise on Coop's face. "Sorry. I didn't realize you were still— I thought—" He scowled. "Look, I'm having an off day. There's a lot of that going around here."

Certain he was referring to Tripp, Amber gave him her full attention. There were lines beside his dark eyes and shadows underneath them. His slacks were wrinkled and hung slightly below his waist. She wondered if he'd eaten or slept. His white shirt needed ironing; his tie was loosened. This smoldering, appealing man could curl her toes and spark her temper. He was closing himself off from her an inch at a time.

Why?

Tamping down a dull ache of foreboding, she asked Tripp, "Ready to show me your clinic?"

He nodded. Again, Amber wondered what he was thinking.

"I'm heading that way, too," Coop said.

They started down the corridor, three astride, Amber in the middle. If Coop hadn't asked a dozen questions about the wedding, the silence would have been palpable.

When they reached the elevator, Amber looked at Tripp. "Have you heard from Montgomery?"

"He called this morning."

"And?" It was like pulling teeth. The elevator started down, and Amber held on to her stomach.

"He thinks the reason he didn't see me at the reception was because things got chaotic after the downpour. He said he spoke with Gentry and Harris, who passed on *my* decision to remain at County General. He thanked me for attending the wedding and wished me well. The man doesn't have a clue he's being completely manipulated."

"You're not going to tell him?"

Tripp shook his head. "I wouldn't know how. And even if I did, I'm not sure he would believe me. It could get ugly, and I've learned to choose my battles."

"Any idea what you're going to do now to fund the clinic?"

The doors slid open and three sets of feet shuffled out. Halfway through the nearly empty lobby, Coop said, "The hospital is hosting a fund-raiser. 'Course, that's like putting a Band-Aid on an amputation."

Amber was the first to reach the fresh outdoors. Behind her, Tripp said, "Your imagery could use a little work today, Cooper."

"At least I didn't say bloody stump."

Amber's laughter floated up, rich and clear. If any one

of them had walked in the other direction, they would have noticed a movement between two vans. If they'd been closer, they might have gotten a whiff of engine grease and sweat and cheap whiskey. Perhaps that would have explained why the hair on the back of Tripp's neck suddenly prickled. It wouldn't have explained the reason for Amber's unease.

Hers was all tied up with Tripp. He hadn't so much as touched her. He'd barely looked at her. Any second now she was going to work up the courage to ask where Coop had gotten the impression that she and Tripp were no longer seeing each other. What did Coop think—that they were just friends? As far as Amber was concerned, they weren't *just* anything.

She got in Tripp's car; Cooper unlocked his. Nobody paid much attention when a rusty van with a broken taillight pulled out of the parking lot and headed west.

Amber's thoughts were elsewhere. Although she could have asked a dozen questions, she remained quiet during the drive. Tripp put on his sunglasses. She lowered the visor, watching the houses go by.

The Mill Creek Medical Clinic was located on the outskirts of town, six or seven blocks from the hospital. She already knew Tripp had paid the city a dollar for an abandoned building that had once housed workers in the logging industry around the turn of the last century. Evidently, the building had been in total disrepair, with boarded-up windows and bats living in the attic and skunks under the rotting porches. She'd gotten a lot of her information from nurses and orderlies at the hospital. Someone—she thought it was Fred—had told her that the clinic was staffed almost completely with volunteers. Nurse Proctor of all people had said that Tripp had cleaned out his savings account to purchase the medical equipment, and he spent most of his wages keeping it running.

Tripp slowed down, pulling into a gravel parking lot in front of the building. She didn't know what she'd expected, but it wasn't the vastness of the house on the hill. She suspended her worries and exclaimed, "It's lovely!"

Amber's simple praise touched Tripp in ways he hadn't expected. Staring out her window, he tried to see it from her perspective. He wouldn't call it lovely, or even majestic. The building couldn't hold a candle to the meticulously restored, ornate Victorian houses lining many of the streets of Ukiah, but as far as he was concerned, his clinic served a more important purpose.

It was sprawling, but well-built and rock solid. He'd patched the roof himself, replaced glass in broken windows, shored up the porches, sanded floors and given the entire building a coat of paint, inside and out.

"No wonder you saw its potential, Tripp. There must be ten rooms on the first floor."

"Eleven."

Her smile was artful and serene. It was as if she approved. It occurred to him that he wanted her approval. A man didn't worry about someone's approval unless he valued that person's opinion. He valued Amber's. He valued her.

It made him as nervous as a schoolboy. But Tripp Calhoun had never been a nervous schoolboy. He'd been rebellious, yes, not to mention a stubborn, arrogant, belligerent, egotistical, troublemaker. But never nervous.

He wanted...

What? Someone to talk to? Sleep with? More?

Whoa. All he was going to do was show her the clinic. The clinic was his top priority, and had to remain that way.

There were only a handful of cars in the gravel lot. Strangely, a rusty van with a broken taillight was blocking both reserved parking spaces. He pulled into an empty spot nearby and was cutting the engine when the van's door opened and a man he'd never seen before got out.

Every nerve in Tripp's body went on red alert. "Amber, stay in the car."

"What? Why?"

"Just do as I say. And lock the doors." He eased his door open and got out.

Coop was already out of his car. His footsteps slowed, then stopped. He was shaking his head at the other man. Tripp couldn't make out exactly what they were saying, but he could tell from the tone of their voices that it wasn't good. The stranger's face was reddened, as if angry, and he laid his hand on a bulge beneath his shirt that was surely a pistol. Coop must have seen it, too. He motioned for Tripp to stay back.

"Can I help you?" Tripp asked.

The man took an ominous step in his direction. "Now, would I be here if I thought you couldn't?"

"Are you sick?" Tripp doubted it, but he was buying time, trying to think.

"I'm sick, all right. Of doctors like you sticking your nose in a man's business." The man was large, with big, beefy, grease-blackened hands, one of which was scratched, with dried blood. His dingy gray T-shirt was sweat-stained, and he reeked of whiskey and cigarette smoke. His complexion was ruddy, his hair the color of dirty dishwater, and in need of a cut and good washing.

"Why don't we go around to the back door?" Tripp said. "I keep a bottle of whiskey inside." He hoped to God that lie didn't turn around and bite him. He wanted to get the guy in front of him. Maybe then he and Coop could take him from behind.

It didn't work. The man didn't budge. "Where is she?"

Tripp tried again. "If you don't want a drink, at least let me take a look at that hand."

This time the ploy worked. The man took his hand off the gun beneath his shirt and studied the scratches. Next, he leered at Tripp. "My hand don't need treatin'. Go on inside. This is between me and Casanova here."

He seemed to think he'd made a joke, because he laughed, a loud, lewd, raucous sound that contained more rage than humor. From the clinic a window squeaked as someone slid it shut, the sound drawing the man's attention. Tripp and Coop only had a moment to exchange a look.

Coop made a gesture with his head. "Go ahead, Dr. Calhoun. Go on in. This is between Ray and me. Ray, why don't you and I step around to the side of the building, out of sight of a patient who might stray past and get in your way?"

With utmost caution, Tripp eased away, toward the porch. Hopefully, Coop would keep the man talking long enough for Tripp to get inside and call the police.

He'd only taken two more steps when a voice stopped him in his tracks. "Darling? You aren't going in without me, are you?"

He looked over his shoulder. Amber was walking jauntily toward him, smiling all around. Tripp swallowed. "I thought you were going to wait in the car."

She stomped her foot and pouted. Tripp's throat convulsed. What the hell was she doing?

"I mean it, Amber. Get back in the car."

"Don't boss me, all right?" She turned to Coop. "He's always bossing me."

Ray glared at Amber. "If you know what's good for you, you'll do what you're told."

Tripp prayed to God Amber would shut up.

She stomped her foot again and stuck out her lower lip. "What I'm told! I'm not a child." Was that her voice, so tiny, so pampered, so damned whiny?

"Amber."

She glanced at Tripp, as if trying to convey something. What the hell was she doing?

With a lift of her chin, she looked at Ray again. "I'll have you know I have every right to go wherever I choose."

"I hate women who think they know everything," Ray spat. "And I hate spoiled rich girls almost as much as that lazy, no-good, lying wench who stole my kids and wants to put me in jail for doing something a real man has the right to do. So if I were you, I'd do what your boyfriend here tells you and shut the hell up."

Two cars drove by, seconds apart. Otherwise, the early evening was quiet. As far as Tripp was concerned, the silence felt ominous, oppressive.

"But I want to see the clinic," Amber said, pouting again. "You both promised to show me." She stepped between Ray and the street, blocking his view of the vehicle that pulled into the lot.

"Amber," Coop said, "why don't you get back in the car, huh? Be a good girl."

She looked at both men. Speaking in an unusually loud, whiny voice, she said, "Oh, all right. Could I at least have the keys so I can listen to the radio?"

Tripp had left the keys in the car. She knew that. What was she—

Suddenly, footsteps pounded behind them and no less than six police officers rushed in from every direction, pistols drawn.

Tripp shoved Amber and Coop behind him.

Ray's hand went to his gun.

"Don't try it," the officer closest shouted.

Another policeman yelled, "Put your hands up where we can see them."

All six officers closed in, pistols pointed. They had Ray facedown on the ground and handcuffed before he knew what hit him. Things moved quickly after that. They read him his rights and stuffed him in the back seat of a cruiser, heading for the county jail.

Two officers remained behind to take statements. Letting Coop handle that, Tripp turned on Amber. "Why didn't you stay in the car?"

Amber's eyes were large now, her voice back to normal as she said, "I was afraid you were going to go inside. And the doors and windows were locked."

"What do you mean they were locked?" He sputtered. "Who locked them, and how could you have known that?"

"Because I told them to. I called the clinic, right after I called 911. Of course, I had to call information for the number. My hands were shaking so hard I could hardly press the right buttons."

The officer confirmed her statement. "She was extremely specific about the procedure. Told us not to use our sirens."

Coop grinned. "Sweetheart, I owe you dinner."

Tripp wasn't smiling. He couldn't. She'd played the spoiled little rich girl very convincingly. But her ingenuous act could have gotten her killed.

Suddenly, he knew what that distant memory that had

been bothering him for the past several days meant. It involved safety.

He couldn't keep a woman like Amber safe.

She'd garnered her knowledge of danger from watching crime dramas on television. She thought that, since this episode had turned out okay, they all would. But Tripp had lived and fought and survived on the city streets. He'd known people who hadn't lived to tell about it. Sure, Ukiah wasn't as dangerous as L.A. But danger was danger and life was a crapshoot. In his world, no matter where it was, Amber would stick out like a sore thumb. It didn't matter that this golden-haired, spoiled, pampered heiress had a heart of gold, nerves of steel and a mind that worked in ways he didn't begin to understand. She would still be a sitting duck. Like his mother had been.

Other than the summer he spent at Hacienda de Alegria, and a few brief affairs like the one with Olivia, he'd been alone most of his life. There was a good reason for that. If he ever found a woman willing to take on the risk of spending her life with him, it would have to be a woman who shared his background and could work behind the scenes or at his side without drawing attention to herself. He'd known that weeks ago, before Amber had breezed into his life and turned it upside down and him with it, making him forget everything except the need running thick and warm through his veins.

Tonight had been one hell of a reminder.

She didn't belong in his world. It didn't have anything to do with prejudice. It had to do with life and death. And Tripp preferred to keep Amber in the first category.

The officers wrote down their names and addresses. Coop went inside to see the patients who were waiting.

True to his word, Tripp showed Amber around as he'd said he would. He spoke in monosyllables.

Amber felt bereft. She'd helped him tonight. They should be celebrating. It wasn't that he was claiming all the glory. He wasn't talking about the episode at all. He had closed himself off even more.

She met a few of the patients, took her tour of the clinic, listened to Tripp's description of each room's use. Every time she looked at the shutters that had come down in Tripp's eyes, she grew more scared. If there was a medicine for heartsickness, she could have used a strong dose.

After the tour, he drove her back to her car. Again, it was executed in nearly complete silence.

Amber didn't much care for complete silence, especially when her heart and future happiness were on the line. "All right, Calhoun, what's the matter?"

"Nothing."

She felt her eyes narrow, but she didn't call him on the carpet about his lie. Instead, she wanted to get him talking. Maybe then, she would be able to figure out what was wrong. "Now that I've seen the clinic," she said, "it's your turn to drive out to see all the changes at the Hopechest Ranch."

His jaw was set, his eyes straight ahead. "Maybe I'll do that sometime."

Her heart thumped erratically. Something snapped inside her, and her patience ran out. "Maybe? Sometime? Could you be a little more vague?"

He finally looked at her, his eyes filling with a curious intensity. For a long moment she looked back at him, hope fluttering in her stomach.

The shutters came back down over his eyes, and

squashed the butterfly wings of her hope. "I don't want to make this more difficult than it already is."

He turned away from her, but she continued looking at him.

As if sensing her gaze, he finally looked at her again. "I don't want to hurt you, Amber."

Meaning he knew exactly what he was doing. She knew the line well. She'd used it herself. He was ditching her.

Scraping together her tattered pride, she closed her mouth and got out of his car. She didn't say another word as she unlocked the Porsche's door. As she turned her key in the ignition. She couldn't help but glance in her rearview mirror. She was weak, her only excuse.

Tripp hadn't moved. He just sat there and let her drive away.

Twelve

The grant application on Amber's desk blurred before her eyes. Resting her chin in her hand, she stared out the window in her office at the Hopechest Foundation, located on the Hopechest Ranch twenty miles from her childhood home in Prosperino. The dynamo director in charge of the center for troubled kids had once said they would all get more done if the administrative building had been built farther from the daily workings of the ranch. Normally, Amber liked it this way. She liked the close proximity to the kids the Foundation was helping. In the past, it had helped with the boredom she constantly fought and made her feel connected to something or someone. Lately, she felt as uprooted as tumbleweed, which was strange, since she was weighted down by a deep-seated sadness.

Some of the older boys staying at the Homestead ambled past on horseback. They were helping the foreman move the herd to greener pastures. She wished she were out there with them. The thought came out of nowhere. She'd been making a lot of wishes lately. This very second, she wished she were anywhere but here. And that was crazy. Her work here was meaningful. Everyone who came here had a purpose. Her purpose was to put the MBA she'd received to good use, helping to run the Foundation her mother had started before everything had gone awry. Now, if only she could concentrate on that work.

She sighed.

It had been a week since she'd seen Tripp. A long, lonely, confusing week. She'd swallowed her pride and called his office. He'd been out. His return call had been cut short by a voice paging him in the background at the hospital. He hadn't called again.

Tears welled in her eyes. She swallowed hard and sighed again. She missed him. She'd tried to be angry. Lord knew it would have been better than this heavy sadness that had settled like a brick in her chest. She couldn't even blame him for seducing her and then tossing her aside. She'd seduced him. She loved him.

"You realize that every time you do that, the roof on this building expands at least a foot before settling back into its rightful place."

Amber stared at the man leaning in her doorway for a full five seconds before she understood that he was referring to her deep sighs. "Hi, Jackson."

Her cousin drew closer. "Those sighs for anybody I know?"

She shrugged and did her best to smile. People were worried about her. Not just any people. Family. Sophie had been the first to notice something was amiss. She must have alerted everyone else. Rand had called again last night. Just when Amber thought there was no cohesion left, the Colton clan pulled together.

Or at least most of them did.

She hadn't slept a wink the first two nights after Tripp had given his little "I don't want to hurt you" speech. She'd been certain that if she concentrated hard enough, she would figure out what had gone wrong. Perhaps if she knew what the problem was, she might understand it. She'd gone over and over everything, and she didn't have a clue. She'd fallen asleep out of sheer exhaustion the third night. And while that hadn't resulted in any insight, either, at least she'd been rested on the fourth day. Rested or not, her emotions were a mess. She'd been bored before Tripp had walked back into her life. She was bored again. But this was worse, for it was accompanied with a sadness she couldn't shake, and a feeling that her life was empty. It wasn't, she knew. She had her work. Why couldn't that be enough?

She sighed.

She missed Tripp. It was that simple. And it really rankled!

"Want to talk about it?" Jackson asked.

"Hmm?" Oh. She'd forgotten she wasn't alone. Chin in hand, she said, "There's not much to talk about."

Jackson made a sound without opening his mouth. Like the rest of the Colton men, he was tall. His jet-black hair and silver-gray eyes had turned the heads of every female juror from eighteen to eighty. Recently, he gave up his job as an attorney with Colton Enterprises, and took a position with the Hopechest Foundation as legal advocate for the kids living at the ranch. His new job agreed with him, but the new warmth in his eyes stemmed from happiness, and his happiness was tied directly to his new wife, Cheyenne. Amber liked Cheyenne, who had believed in Jackson and in his innocence as only a woman completely in love could.

Amber now understood that kind of love. Tears sprang out of nowhere, but she blinked them back.

Jackson took a seat across from her desk. His gaze was steady, his voice compassionate as he said, "If there's one thing Cheyenne has taught me about women, it's that when one of you says there's not much to talk about, there's usually a lot to talk about. It's just not easy, is it?"

Amber almost smiled.

"That's more like it," he said.

"I appreciate your support, Jackson, but I really don't know what to say."

"You're not ill?"

"Not physically. No."

"Is something going on with your mother?"

"Nothing's changed there."

"Then this must involve a man."

She sighed.

And he said, "Anybody I know?"

"You remember Tripp Calhoun?"

Jackson leaned back in his chair and folded his arms as if settling in for the duration. Now that Amber had started it, it looked as if she was going to have to finish it. She caught her sigh in the nick of time.

"I always thought Tripp was a good man," Jackson said. "Was I wrong?"

"No."

"I take it you've been seeing him?"

She nodded. "I was."

"Ah. Past tense. And you love him. Present tense."

Tears sprang to her eyes again. Oh, but that was getting

annoying. "How I feel doesn't matter, because he doesn't love me in return."

"I find that hard to believe."

Her laughter sounded slightly hysterical, but it made her feel a little better. "Believe it or not, he doesn't."

"How do you know?"

"Trust me, I know." She stared at the application for a grant from an organization in New York. The group needed financial assistance to help fund a day-care center for kids who were HIV positive. There were so many wonderful causes. She wished the foundation had enough money to help every one who requested support, let alone someone who just happened to be too stubborn to even ask. Which brought her to her next point.

"Not only does he not love me, but it's pretty obvious that he doesn't trust me. He started a health-care clinic for the needy in and around Ukiah. He runs it on a shoe-string, sacrificing everything for its success. I would love to help. But does he apply for a grant? Oh, no. Not the fierce and proud Dr. Tripp Calhoun."

She paused long enough to take a breath. Realizing how she sounded, she pulled a face. Jackson looked at her as if seeing her turn into a ranting lunatic was an everyday occurrence. It wasn't. She only turned into one where Tripp was concerned. "I get a little carried away."

"Would obtaining a grant from the Foundation be a feasible solution to his clinic's financial troubles?"

"Oh, yes, it would be a feasible solution."

"And yet Tripp hasn't applied."

She was a little slower to shake her head this time.

"Would you say Tripp is a bright man?" He held up one hand. "Where business is concerned, at least?"

She nodded again.

"And yet he hasn't contacted the foundation on behalf of his clinic."

She didn't even bother to shake her head.

"Think he has a reason for failing to ask you for money?"

She leaned back in her chair and covered her mouth with both hands. Her heart was taking turns speeding up and slowing down, but her mind raced.

Did Tripp have a reason?

She recalled two separate instances when she'd told him that the men in her past only wanted her family's money. One of those times had been immediately after they'd made love, for heaven's sake.

No wonder he hadn't applied. Or called. Or continued to see her. He cared about her. She knew how little sense that made, but this was Tripp she was dealing with.

"Do you think everyone has this much trouble with love, Jackson?"

"I don't know about the rest of the population, but it seems that anybody named Colton does. It may be more trouble for us, but in the end, it's worth it." With that, he rose to his feet. Leaving her alone with her thoughts and revelations, he returned to his office down the hall.

Amber jumped up and paced to the door, to the window, back and forth and back and forth. The fog was clearing from her brain much the way it had thinned into transparency when she was driving to work this morning. She could think more coherently now. She'd given up on Tripp without a fight. Normally, she didn't give up so easily. She wasn't afraid of hard work, professionally or personally. But she was inexperienced in matters of the heart. It made her feel vulnerable and as unsteady as the brand-new filly trying out her legs for the first time in the pasture by the barns.

Although she and Tripp hadn't exchanged words of love, he had been a caring lover in Mississippi. He'd been ardent and passionate at her place right after, too. And then, in a flash, something had changed.

What?

She glanced at the phone, and then at her cluttered desk full of work waiting for her undivided attention. It seemed unlikely that Tripp was going to call. And she couldn't concentrate on work anyway. Perhaps it was time she paid him a little visit and demanded a few answers.

"Going someplace?" Jackson asked as she passed his open door, a sheaf of papers in her hand.

"Darn right I am. It's high time somebody makes a certain stubborn doctor see reason."

Jackson said something encouraging that Amber didn't stick around long enough to hear.

"Oh, señorita! You must be my replacement! Thank goodness you are here."

Amber looked around. There were several patients in the waiting room. The heavyset woman with the thick Spanish accent appeared to be talking to her.

"Come," she called. "I will tell you what to do."

Amber closed the door and sauntered closer. Tripp hadn't been at the hospital. Fred, the flirtatious orderly, had been pretty sure he was at his clinic this afternoon.

She'd hurried over, and sure enough, his car was among the handful of vehicles in the lot. She'd decided to take that as a good sign. She wasn't certain what to think about the Spanish woman behind the counter who was talking a mile a minute.

"Thank goodness you are early. My granddaughter is

sick and I must go home. Come. I will explain what to do. Do not worry. It is a piece of cake.''

The woman rattled off instructions regarding the phone, an antiquated filing system and a roomful of patients. "Do you have any questions?"

Amber peered toward the hallway leading to several closed doors. "Is Dr. Calhoun on duty?"

"*Si.* He is a gift, that one."

"A gift horse," Amber muttered under her breath.

"Pardon?"

"Oh, it was nothing. Never mind. Goodbye. And good luck with your granddaughter."

Huffing slightly, the woman, whose name was still unknown to Amber, reached for her purse and hurried out the door, her loose-fitting dress fluttering as she went.

The phone rang the instant the door closed. A girl who looked too young to have a baby of her own stared at Amber over the top of an infant's dark head. Chubby-cheeked twins cried from their father's lap, while two other children fought over a toy in the corner. An old man glared at Amber as if the ringing phone and all the noise was somehow her fault.

She didn't know what to do about the rest, but she knew how to put an end to the ringing. She grabbed up the phone. "Mill Creek Medical Clinic."

Winging it, she scanned the appointment book, jotted information. The phone rang again seconds later. She held a baby, fished a toy from behind a row of chairs and struck up a conversation with the crotchety old man. She'd never been in such dire need of more hands. She was still determined that her confrontation with Tripp was going to take place. In the meantime, there was plenty of work to do.

* * *

Amber's hair was tumbling out of its clasp, a corner of her blouse was untucked and one shoulder was wet with one of the twins' drool by the time she instructed the last patient to go on through to the examination rooms. The phones had finally stopped ringing and nearly everyone had gone home. She used the relative quiet to organize the desk and tried to decide what she would say to Tripp.

She had nearly finished straightening the waiting area and was reading the flyer on the wall, advertising the fund-raising dance being hosted by the hospital in a couple of weeks, when she heard a sound behind her. She turned slowly. Tripp stood at the other end of the room. Everything about him was dark, his hair, pants, even his eyes, darkened by an unreadable emotion. Amber's heart fluttered twice, then rose up to her throat.

"What are you doing?" he asked.

She'd had warmer welcomes at Macy's. She gestured to the magazines she'd been straightening. "I'm working."

"You don't work here."

"You know what they say about being in the right place at the right time."

Apparently, he failed to see the humor. "Where's Rosa?"

So that was the woman's name. "She had to leave. Her granddaughter was sick."

The last patient of the day came out into the waiting room, her six-month-old baby asleep on her shoulder. Anna Garcia smiled tiredly. Closer to sixteen than twenty-one, the single mother patted her baby's small back. "Thank you, Dr. Calhoun."

Hearing his mother's voice, the baby opened his eyes and began to suck his little thumb. Content and secure, his eyes fluttered closed once again. Amber thought Anna looked equally as tired. She always wished there were more she could do to help in situations like these.

The girl dug into the pocket of her baggy jeans. Placing several coins on the counter, she started for the door. Amber opened her mouth to call her back, but Tripp silenced her with a stern look.

The door closed. And she and Tripp were alone. At last.

His mouth set in annoyance. Obviously he wasn't as happy about that as she was. And yet she swore his eyes were drinking her up.

"It's been a long day," he said. "And I have rounds to make at the hospital."

Subtle, he wasn't. Amber strode to the checkout area, where she counted three dollars and eighty-six cents in loose change. Dropping the coins into the drawer, she said, "This isn't enough money to buy bandages for the clinic, but it would have been enough to buy a loaf of bread or a gallon of milk for Anna and her baby."

An unwelcome tension coiled tighter in Tripp's stomach. He hadn't paid much attention when four-year-old Jose Martinez mentioned a golden angel in the waiting room. It wasn't until an hour later, when old Samuel DeWitt described the new volunteer that Tripp realized they were talking about Amber. His breathing had been unsteady ever since.

Eyeing the loose tendrils of her hair and the mascara smudges under her eyes, he finally said, "Anna's proud. By paying what she felt she could afford, this isn't charity."

"Then it's a matter of pride?"

He glanced around the room. He was pretty sure he knew what Amber was asking, and uncertain how to reply. He'd tried to put an end to this a week ago. He didn't want to hurt her, but he didn't think there was any other way to ensure that she took no for an answer.

"I appreciate everything you've tried to do for me, Amber."

For about a millisecond, he saw hope in her eyes. Leaning down, she retrieved her large purse from the floor near the filing cabinet, then busied herself riffling through a sheaf of papers inside.

"But it isn't a good idea for you to come here."

She straightened, her green eyes delving his, her throat convulsing as her hope gave way to something a lot less pleasant. He was getting through to her. It would have been nice if he didn't feel like something he'd stepped in. He had damn good reasons for ending this. He cursed his body for wanting something it had no business wanting.

She glanced down at a newspaper clipping attached to the top of a sheaf of papers. "You probably don't read the society pages. It seems that Olivia Babcock and Derek Spencer have set a date."

Being careful not to touch her, he accepted the papers from her. "What's all this?" he asked.

"It's everything you'll need to apply for a grant from the Hopechest Foundation. There's an application in the packet, along with specific guidelines. Follow them to the letter. You'll need to supply a statement of need, your financial information, earnings, wages, expenses, as well as documentation on how the clinic will positively affect the people in the area. It will have to be reviewed by the board, and there are no guarantees, but I see no reason for them not to offer some assistance."

He stood perfectly still. "You don't have to do this, Amber. Not for me."

She met his gaze bravely, but he wasn't fooled.

"I'm doing it for Jose and Anna and Manuel and hundreds of others like them."

Tripp had never come across a woman he understood less and who drew him more. He was trying to make it clear to her that what they'd shared was over and she was still offering her family's money. "You're an amazing woman."

If the situation weren't so serious, the face she made would have been comical.

He ran a hand through his hair. It was short now, only one of the things that had changed this past month. He had changed, too, but reality hadn't. That episode with the wife-beater had driven that fact home.

"One of these days," he said, "you're going to make some lucky man very happy."

Amber stared at Tripp for several seconds while her heart cracked open a little further. She refused to whimper. Some lucky man? Gee. What a sweet thing to say. And so original.

Her temper flared, a definite improvement over despair. "What type of man should I be looking for? In your knowledgeable opinion, I mean."

Surely, her sarcasm wasn't lost on him, but he didn't get angry as she'd expected. Instead, he almost smiled. It nearly broke her heart the rest of the way.

"Someone like you. Someone good and smart and funny and kind. A man of wealth and culture. He's going to need patience. And stamina." When he spoke again, his voice was huskier. "And he'd better know how to argue, because you'd get bored with someone who can't hold his own in any discussion."

He knew her so well. She could have cried. This was it. He was ending it. He didn't want her. Or at least he wasn't going to allow himself to have her, or anyone like her. Curious, she said, "What about you? What sort of woman would you look for?"

"Coop said it pretty well when he called me a loner. If I ever do decide to search for a wife, it will most likely be someone of Latino descent. Someone who will fit in in my world."

"There's only one planet, one world, Tripp, and we're already both living in it."

"Are we?" The shutters came down over his eyes again. "In the future, I would appreciate it if you would stay away from places where danger could be lurking."

Something about that last statement lodged in her mind. He didn't want her anywhere near danger. She recalled the way he'd reacted when that car had backfired moments before Rand had called last Sunday. Now that she thought about it, it wasn't the phone call that had interrupted their lovemaking. It had been that sudden, loud noise. It had sounded a little like a gunshot.

Watching as he locked cabinets, she was close to putting it all together. He turned out more lights, bolted the back door and the windows.

"Thank you again for all your help, Amber. Give my best to your father."

Amber didn't know what to say. She'd come for answers, but she was being dismissed. She sensed that he cared about her, but she couldn't get through to him. What else could she do to change his mind? Beaten, she settled her purse under her arm and started for the door.

"Amber?"

Hope surged. "Yes?"

"I'd like your word that you'll stay away from the clinic."

She stared at him for interminable seconds, not moving, not blinking, not breathing. Finally, she drew herself up to her full height and turned on her heel. Instead of giving him her word, she gave the door a loud slam.

Silas "Snake Eyes" Pike stepped quietly from the shadows on Main Street in Keyhole, Wyoming. His hand shook as he patted the empty pocket where he normally kept a flask for emergencies. Ever since that witch, Meredith Colton had cut off his money supply, he'd been forced to remain sober.

Being careful of his step, he ambled across the street toward Summer's Autumn Antiques. What a one-horse town this had turned out to be. None of the bars would let him run up a tab. He hadn't even been able to hire a hooker to take the edge off his shakes.

Things were looking up, though. He'd tried watching that young punk Sheriff Toby Atkins. The man led the life of a monk. After a couple of days keeping the lily-hearted sheriff under surveillance, Silas had decided to scope out Wyatt and Annie Russell. The Russells, Wyatt in particular, had connections to the Colton family. Silas didn't trust him as far as he could throw him.

He'd heard from one of his drinking buddies that the Russells had befriended a girl with hair an unusual shade of red. Chestnut colored, he'd called it. It so happened Emily Blair had chestnut-colored hair. Silas was playing a hunch that the Russells were somehow involved with Emily's sudden and untimely disappearance.

He'd bet his next drink that they knew where she was hiding. It was up to Silas to get one of them to spill the beans. He'd been watching the place for three days. Who better to spill the beans than the pair of red-haired boys who took their huge monster of a black dog for a walk to the corner every day when they got home from the nursery school or kindergarten or wherever the hell they spent the morning?

Today, Silas was ready for them. He ambled out of one of many tourist traps lining Main Street just as the boys neared. Peering through the wire-rimmed bifocals he'd lifted off an unsuspecting old man yesterday, Silas smiled at the boys. "Mornin', fellers. Oh, looky there. Guess it's afternoon, huh?"

The boys were identical, right down to their cowlicks and suspicious stares. Their big black dog bared his teeth.

"That's a big dog you have there. What's his name?"

The children each placed a hand on the dog's broad back. The boy on the right said, "His name's Chopper. Are you a stranger? Cuz we're not s'posed to talk to strangers."

Silas tugged at the waistband of the polyester pants he'd gotten in the Dumpster behind the Salvation Army store. "I guess that depends. I'm a grandpaw. Are grandpaws strangers?"

The boys conferred the point over the top of the dog's broad back. "Guess not," the designated talker of the two declared.

Silas commended himself on his brilliant disguise. He'd had to shave off his Fu-Manchu style mustache, and he'd taken white shoe polish to his hair and eyebrows. The mustache would grow back and the shoe polish would wash out. It had been worth it. The boys fell for it hook, line and sinker. The dog was another matter. That was okay. Silas didn't need the dog to trust him. He only needed to get the kids talking.

"Me'n Noah don't have a grandpa. We have a new dad, though."

Silas knew all about the boys' new father. Wyatt Russell, the fancy-ass attorney from D.C. had proven to be a thorn in his side.

Reaching a hand into his pocket, Silas brought out a tattered photo. The step he took toward the boys was cut short by their dog's low, menacing growl. "That's a good watchdog you have there. This here's my granddaughter…" Silas had to think fast. "…Penny."

"She looks just like Emily," the quieter of the boys exclaimed.

"Who?" Silas asked, all false innocence.

"Our friend, Emily."

He'd purposefully chosen an old photograph of Emily Blair. "This here's Penny. She's fifteen. Best darn granddaughter in the world. She and her mama moved to Texas a while back."

"Emily moved, too."

"You don't say? She move to Texas, too?"

"Nope. To Montana."

"Yeah?" Silas said, getting dizzy from looking through the bifocals. "I went to Montana once." Making certain the photo faced out, he tucked it back into his pocket. His hand shook. He really needed a drink. Both boys seemed to be mesmerized by his movements. "Were 'bouts does she live in Montana?"

"She lives in Red—"

"Noah! Alex!"

The children turned around at the sound of their mother's voice. Silas slipped inside the sporting goods store, and quietly out the back door.

Life was a crapshoot, no doubt about that. They didn't call him Snake Eyes for nothing. Course, rolling a pair of ones wasn't easy, unless the dice were weighted, that is. Then, it was almost as easy as getting information out of a couple of snot-nosed red-haired little boys.

Silas stuffed the floppy-rimmed fishing cap and bifocals into the first trash can he came to. Cutting through another back alley, he made his way back to the room he was renting by the day. He had packing to do. Emily Blair was in Montana, in a town called Red-something.

Silas "Snake Eyes" Pike was as good as on his way.

Patsy let the door slam as she rushed through it. "Teddy! Joey!" She shaded her eyes with her hand, searching the gardens for her darlings. The boys were nowhere in sight. But Amber was sitting out by the pool, talking to her father. Sulking.

Patsy shuddered with distaste. "Joe!" she said to the man she'd pretended to be married to for ten long years. "Where have the boys run off to this time? They had better not be mucking out stalls in the barns!"

The boys, eight and ten years old, came running out of the house, Joe, Jr. in the lead, his younger brother in hot pursuit. Patsy beamed as they each did a cannonball into the pool. Her darlings were right here in the garden. If only she could find the baby she lost all those years ago, her life would be nearly complete. There was still the issue of getting rid of Joe and that pesky Emily, but one thing at a time.

Two days ago, she'd received word from the private investigator that a baby girl fitting her baby's description had been involved in a black-market adoption, handled by a shady doctor in Stockton. The records indicated that the baby had gone to live with a couple in Ohio. Patsy had been trying to get that child back all her life. She'd urged the investigator to continue the search.

She wondered what her child, a grown woman now, would look like. Surely, Patsy thought, her eyes narrowing, her lip curling, she wouldn't act anything like either

of Meredith's grown daughters, who were both so sickeningly sweet it was all Patsy could do not to retch when
she saw them.

"Joe, I need to talk to you."

He spoke to Amber and, laying a hand on her shoulder,
rose to his feet and started toward Patsy. His eyes iced
over the closer he came. She bet there hadn't been cold-
ness in his eyes when he'd been talking to that simpering
Amber. Oh, the things she'd been forced to endure.

"What is she doing here?"

Joe Colton studied the woman his beautiful Meredith
had become. If it wasn't for Joe, Jr. and Teddy, he would
have left his beloved home a long time ago. Hacienda de
Alegria, House of Joy, was a lie, one that was growing
increasingly difficult to live. "She's our daughter. This
is her home."

"Must she sulk?"

"She's hurting."

Patsy rolled her eyes and dismissed Amber's problems
with a wave of her hand.

Joe said, "You could show a little compassion."

"Don't be so melodramatic. She's twenty-six years
old. Let her sulk at her own place. You've spoiled them
all rotten. Amber and Sophie are both just like M—"
She clamped her mouth shut.

"Who? Not you."

"No, not me. I'm not weak or simpering."

Joe looked at those pursed lips. There was a time he
couldn't get enough of them. There was a time when he'd
loved everything about this woman. Now, he only loved
the memory of what she'd once been.

"What did you want, Meredith?"

Her lips thinned as if in aversion. "Never mind. I'll
do it myself."

Shrugging his shoulders, he ambled to the pool area where he'd been talking to Amber. "Let me get you something cool to drink, pumpkin."

Behind him, Patsy heard the endearment. Pumpkin, my eye. How dare he call that simpering little brat a pet name, after looking at *her* with open loathing! He'd probably never looked at Meredith like that. Oh, no, he would have only looked at Meredith with warmth and affection. Ha! He would never look at her that way again. Patsy took comfort in that, and in the theory that Meredith had probably become a homeless person and had died as a Jane Doe. Still, nearly saying that Sophie and Amber were exactly like Meredith had been a close one. She had to be more careful.

She was overwrought, that was all. She couldn't help it. Any second now the phone was going to ring, and Silas Pike was going to have more news regarding Emily's whereabouts. Silas had called a few days ago with the news that he had it from a very reliable source that the snotty little orphan had left Wyoming. Maybe the man wasn't completely inept after all. As soon as he discovered which direction she'd gone, he would close in on her, and Patsy was at once excited and nervous. It was no wonder she was having a difficult time keeping up the charade.

Her private cell phone rang, startling her. Taking it from the pocket of her exquisitely styled jacket, she placed it to her ear. "Yes?"

"I think I know where she is."

A smile sprang to her lips. Fortuitously, she glanced in the direction Joe had gone. Both he and Amber had turned to look at her. "Hello, Sharon!" she said loudly. "You've found the perfect bag, you say? You're sure it's the right one?"

Silas kept his voice very quiet on the other end. "I have it from two very reliable sources that our little Emily Blair is in Montana. I'm narrowing down where as we speak."

"But that's wonderful." Patsy glanced at the pool where her darlings were playing. A burst of excitement tore through her.

"I'll call as soon as I know anything."

"Yes, yes. I'm sure you are thrilled. I know how difficult finding the right accessory can be." She lowered her voice. "You'd better not screw this up again." Raising the volume again, she said, "I look forward to hearing all about it."

She turned off the phone and schooled her expression into a smooth mask. Finally, everything was falling into place. The investigator would find her long-lost daughter. She had her precious sons. And soon, Emily would be silenced forever.

"I've invited Amber to stay for dinner, Meredith," Joe called from the chaise longue near the pool.

Patsy paused on her way inside, and cast Joe an annoyed look. "Tell Inez, not me. Keep an eye on the boys."

Amber stared until her mother disappeared inside.

"I'm sorry, pumpkin. She's been extra distraught and distant lately."

Amber met her father's gaze, and it was all she could do to keep tears out of her eyes at what she saw in the depth of his. The sadness in her father's gaze could only have come from a lonely heart. The loneliest of the lonely.

"It's all right, Dad. It isn't your fault."

Joe rose to his feet. "Is it? Any of it? What could I have done differently?"

"Hey, Dad!" Joe, Jr. called. "Look at me!"

Joe and Amber both watched as the boy with the lean, lanky build did another cannonball into the pool. Teddy swam up behind Joe and dunked his older brother. A series of screeches and boyish laughter ensued. It seemed that even the evening songbirds stopped to watch the tussle. The boys were happy, or at least relatively so. Amber believed that, if not for them, their dad would have left their mother years ago. But they needed him, for without his influence, she would surely smother them.

Sighing, she rose, too. "Bye, guys!" she called to her little brothers.

"Bye, Amber!"

"See ya!"

Her dad said, "You're leaving?"

She nodded. "I think it's best, Dad."

"I'm worried about you, Amber."

She reached up and kissed his lean cheek. She didn't tell him not to worry, because she knew he would anyway. But as she left Hacienda de Alegria, she was worried, too. Seeing her mother and father together always made her sad. They used to be so happy, so much in love. What could have happened to change her mother so?

Starting her car, she drove through the wrought-iron gates, and left Hacienda de Alegria behind. The flyer announcing the fund-raiser for Tripp's clinic fluttered on the seat next to her. Turning on the air conditioner, she pressed a button, putting up the windows. Pointing her car toward Fort Bragg, she wondered how her father stood it. It was difficult to sustain true love, and impossible to sustain the artificial kind.

She'd truly come to understand that recently, because her love for Tripp was true. It had only been a few days

since she'd paid him that little visit at his clinic. She
could picture so clearly the open longing in his eyes. And
yet he'd had the nerve to dismiss her, and request that
she not return. It was too dangerous, he'd claimed. And
then, as if that wasn't bad enough, he'd proceeded to
describe the perfect man for her.

Amber brought her car to a stop at a red light. Her
thoughts came to a similar halt.

Danger. There was that word that had lodged in the
back of her mind. Tripp had been furious when she'd
gotten involved with the capture of that man who'd
beaten his wife. He'd overreacted when that car had
backfired when they'd arrived home from Mississippi.

If he had his way, he would keep her up on a shelf,
safe.

Who did he think he was? For years she'd done whatever she could to earn people's love. She'd attended Radcliffe because her mother had wanted her to. She went
into the family business because her father wanted her
to. Finally, she'd believed she'd found someone whose
love was unconditional. And he wanted to keep her safe,
even if it meant they couldn't be together.

Horns honked behind her. Amber turned her attention
to her surroundings. The light had turned green and she
started through.

Tripp loved her. The thought came, like an epiphany.
He loved her. Okay, he had a strange way of showing it,
but he loved her. Why else would he be so worried about
her? Why else would he sacrifice what they shared in the
name of keeping her safe?

He loved her. And she loved him, and somebody had
darn well better not give up on them.

He thought he knew her so well. He even thought he
knew what kind of man she should look for. She stopped

at the next traffic light and picked up the flyer. The fund-raiser was scheduled for the middle of August, two weeks away.

She had an idea.

By the time she pulled into her driveway in Fort Bragg, she had a full-scale plan. She had two weeks to work out the details.

Come hell or high water, she was going to show one Tripp Calhoun that he'd picked the wrong girl to put up on a shelf.

Thirteen

"**R**elax, Calhoun. And smile. This is a fund-raiser, not a funeral."

Tripp slid a finger between his neck and the starched collar of his white shirt and scowled at his friend. "Look who's talking."

It was true. Gavin Cooper was every bit as edgy as Tripp, and had been for days. Both men's unease stemmed from members of the opposite sex. The woman giving Coop trouble was the journalist from the local newspaper, who had arrived at the cotillion an hour ago.

Tripp gritted his teeth. Who heard of cotillions in this day and age? The fund-raiser was supposed to be a casual dance, dammit, and had been until Amber had gotten involved in the preparations. Suddenly, it had become a cotillion, complete with formal invitations and media coverage that reached all the way to San Francisco.

Several of Tripp's patients had been interviewed, but

none had captured the media's attention like little P.J. Pattison, the curly-haired boy whose arm had been injured in the car accident that had claimed his mother's life. Now in foster care, continuing his rehab, and still a patient at the clinic, P.J. had become the Mill Creek Medical Clinic's poster child. His picture, along with his new puppy, compliments of Fred the orderly, had graced the papers and was tacked on lampposts and telephone poles in every small town and large city in northern California. Due to the publicity, there was now a long list of loving couples who wanted to adopt the little boy. Which was all fine and good.

What wasn't fine and good was the publicity Tripp had received. A normal man didn't get this famous unless he died, got arrested or won the lottery. Not even then.

He couldn't blame Amber for that, though God knew he'd tried. Somehow, a nosy journalist had gotten wind of Coop's and Tripp's confrontation with that wife batterer. A veritable media frenzy had ensued. He and Coop had been dubbed the heroes of Ukiah County General in general, and Mill Creek Medical Clinic in particular. Donations were pouring in from all over the state. So far, Tripp had received four marriage proposals from women he'd never even met, Coop, five. The journalist who'd covered the story, however, whom Coop was openly pursuing, would have nothing to do with him.

Coop shook his head, his gaze following the short, dark-haired woman's progress across the room. "Jenna Maria Tribiano. A woman with three names always spells trouble." Coop remained quiet for a time, then said, "Okay, I know what my problem is. What's yours?"

There was a question, Tripp thought. But the truth was, he didn't know what the hell was wrong with him.

He took a deep breath. And smelled Amber's perfume.

His mind shut down and his heart sped up. Her scent had been haunting him for two weeks. Since there wasn't an heiress with golden hair nearby, he brought his wrist closer to his nose and took a whiff. It seemed her scent had indelibly permeated the expensive fibers.

It was everywhere he went, lingering in the corridors and in the elevator at Ukiah County General and in the waiting room at the clinic. He'd told her to stay away from the clinic. That woman didn't take orders well. Oh, she'd made certain their paths didn't cross, volunteering at the clinic only when he was on duty at the hospital, then coming to the hospital when he was at the clinic. Other than the glimpse he'd caught of her shiny red sports car leaving the hospital parking lot as he was pulling up, he hadn't seen her in two weeks. Not quite seeing her, yet knowing he might at any given moment, was driving him to distraction.

"Red alert at two o'clock," Coop said under his breath. "Check out that dress!"

A buzz went through the crowd as every man between eighteen and eighty did exactly that. Amber stood beneath the arch at one end of the pavilion, fashionably late, probably by design. Her hair was a tumble of curls around her neck and shoulders, her dress the stuff fantasies were made of. X-rated fantasies.

"Who's the guy she's with?" Coop asked.

Forcing his fingers out of the fists they'd automatically made at his sides, Tripp wondered that himself.

"That's some red dress," Coop said. "What it covers is almost as intriguing as what it doesn't."

"I thought you were madly in love with your journalist."

The man touted as the Don Juan of County General

gave Tripp a sidelong glance. "Since when did being in love keep a man from looking at other women?"

Which probably had something to do with the reason the journalist was having nothing to do with Coop. Music wafted from the bandstand near the pavilion. The city of Ukiah had graciously offered to host the cotillion in the city park. The sun was going down, the million or so white lights someone had strung through the trees and under the eaves of several buildings, including the open structure where people were dancing, were starting to twinkle elegantly.

On the other side of the pavilion, Amber took a deep breath. Nerves fluttered in her stomach. She'd attended events such as this one all her life. Therefore, her nerves had to be coming from some other source. She nodded at something her date said, and glanced around the structure. Her gaze collided with Tripp's, then held. No wonder she was nervous. He was looking at her. No, glaring was more accurate.

The extravaganza had begun at seven. She'd heard it was already a resounding success. That pleased her. But it wasn't the only reason she'd gone to so much trouble these past two weeks. She was going to open Tripp's eyes, or die trying. She introduced her date to the chairman of the board of the hospital, then accepted an invitation to dance. When someone else asked her, she accepted that as well.

She noticed that Tripp seemed to be filling his time watching her. Finally, Jan Sprague, a nurse from OB, practically dragged him onto the dance floor. When the song ended, he and Jan danced another one, this one more lively. Jan excused herself before he asked her for a third dance. Amber found herself shoulder to shoulder with Tripp along the floor's edge.

"I thought ladies didn't wear red."

She'd rehearsed several scenarios in her mind. In them, Tripp had been distant, quiet, sulky or aloof. His anger surprised her.

"Does my dress bother you?" she asked. The way his mouth was set indicated that he'd passed bothered awhile ago. "I believe what I said was that a woman whose fiancée, pretend or otherwise, was trying to secure a position in an upscale medical practice should appear demure and charming, and shouldn't try to outshine the head pediatrician's wife."

Tripp didn't bother replying. Obviously, there was nothing wrong with her memory. There was nothing wrong with his, either, dammit. He was trying hard not to remember how she'd felt in his arms, how her skin had felt, tasted, how her sighs had sounded, how her pleasure had become his.

"Care to dance with somebody who knows how it's done, Amber?" a young man said close to her ear.

She smiled affectionately and placed her hand in the crook of Fred's arm. Tripp remained rooted to the spot, seething. When the song ended, Fred returned her where he'd found her, then ambled on to his next conquest.

Tripp said, "You're robbing the cradle, aren't you?"

With a lift of her chin, she stuck her nose in the air and breezed away. Obviously, she knew her etiquette, but she only took civility so far.

She was trouble. He'd known it the first time he'd laid eyes on her a month ago when she'd been wearing that damned purple bikini. Still, he had something to say to her, and he didn't appreciate her cold shoulder.

She'd helped herself to a glass of punch. Easing closer, he did the same.

"The fund-raiser for your clinic seems to be a resounding success."

There was no sense wondering how she'd known he was behind her. "At least you still think of it as my clinic."

She turned slightly, the lift of her left eyebrow the only indication she gave that she'd heard the sarcasm in his voice. It was his clinic, dammit. He should have a say in who volunteered there. But no. She breezed in whenever she pleased, just as she'd breezed into his fund-raiser, just as she continuously invaded his dreams.

"You look tired, Tripp."

He scowled. Of course he looked tired. He was getting no sleep and even less satisfaction.

"I've given what you said careful consideration." It was his turn to look perplexed. So she clarified. "Regarding the type of man I should marry."

"And?" he prodded.

"And, I've accepted lunch dates with a few different men these past two weeks."

"How many is a few?" He clamped his mouth shut and jerked his gaze away before he could glimpse the knowing smile she was trying valiantly to keep off her face.

"Three actually. The first was a plastic surgeon from Boston."

"Sounds perfect for you."

"In many ways he probably was."

Tripp picked up on the "was" right away.

"He's wealthy and has a pedigree you wouldn't believe. He received his education in England, loves opera and Shakespeare."

"Have you set a date?"

The roll of her eyes was hardly proper. "He bored me

silly. But I will say this for him. He taught me something about myself."

They must have started walking when they'd started talking, because the music wafting on the warm, moist air was coming from a distance, and people moving about at the gala blurred slightly beneath the relative darkness of the little white lights.

"And what's that?" Tripp feigned nonchalance.

"I don't want to spend my life with a man who makes a fortune giving rich women plastic boobs and perfect noses," she replied. "It turns out the second man is a friend of Fred's. I know, I know." She held up a hand before he could say anything. "I, too, would prefer if the man I marry were old enough to vote. Of course, if I truly loved him, that wouldn't matter."

Tripp conceded the point. "And the third?"

"A biker with hair longer than yours used to be and a tattoo of a cobra covering his entire back."

"Are you crazy? Don't you know how dangerous that could be?"

Tripp never saw the stomp she gave his foot coming. Pain shot up his leg, vibrating inside his shoe.

"He's a nice guy who happens to like long hair and doesn't mind pain. He works at the animal shelter and cries when they play the national anthem. But that isn't the point."

Tripp wasn't altogether sure he was going to like her point, but if she didn't get to it pretty soon, he was going to haul her into his arms and kiss her. The thought came out of nowhere, heating his blood. And ticking him off. So he said, "I'm sure he loves his mother, too. Do you know how many men on death row profess to love their mothers, Amber? What about the guy you're with to-night?"

She poked a finger into his chest hard enough to rival the pain in his foot. "Philip happens to already be engaged. To my friend, Claire."

"Then why did you bring him with you?"

"To prove a point, you big lummox. I can take care of myself. None of those men can keep me safe any more than you can." At his dumbfounded expression, she said, "That's right. You can't keep me safe. And guess what? I can't keep you safe, either. Almost twenty years ago, my brother was killed riding his bike in the safest neighborhood in the country. Tragedy can happen anywhere, and does, all right?"

"You don't understand, Amber."

"Oh, don't you dare tell me that. I understand plenty, no thanks to you. You closed yourself off to me and any explanations as to your peculiar behavior."

"Pecu—"

"I'm not finished. You can refuse to work with me. You can even refuse to see me. But you can't keep me safe. And since we're on the subject, I've had it with trying to earn people's love and acceptance. From now on, I'm going to do what I want. I've received more satisfaction volunteering in the clinic these past two weeks than I've received doing anything my entire life." She paused a moment. "Well, almost anything. What do you say about that?"

He captured her hand before she poked a hole through his chest. "I say that for a pampered heiress, you have a lot of spunk."

The eyes she raised to his were big and green and watery, her face, suddenly pale. Her lips quivered, and before he understood the reason, she said, "Go to hell, Tripp," then spun around and rushed away from him.

He had to hurry, limping, to catch up. "Amber, wait."

She shook off his hand, but at least she came to a stop. "I suppose I should thank you."

He noticed she didn't, though. "For what?"

Her eyes on something in the distance, she said, "I've discovered what true love is this summer." Her chin went up huffily. "Guess there's no accounting for taste after all."

Tripp figured he had that coming, and then some. "I could thank you, too."

"What for, pray tell?"

He gestured to the extravaganza. "For this. And for the grant. I've applied for a dozen others. And I received an interesting phone call from Montgomery Perkins." The older doctor had pledged an obscene amount of money, which Tripp had accepted graciously. But that wasn't what he was talking about. "It seems a waiter at the restaurant in Mississippi saw us leave the rehearsal dinner. He told Cornelia that I never laid a hand on Derek Spencer. Perkins called Spencer on the carpet over it. To make a long story short, Spencer's position has been revoked. He'll be lucky to get a job changing bedpans. Montgomery offered the position to me."

Amber's mouth dropped open, her eyes large as she whispered, "What did you tell him?"

"I turned him down."

"But—"

"I don't want to move to Santa Rosa."

"Why not?"

He shrugged. "Until about two minutes ago, I didn't know. Now I know. It's because you aren't there."

For a moment, he thought she was softening. But then her back and shoulders straightened. "I don't like what I do for a living. I only went into it to try to win my mother's approval, and I suppose in a sense, my father's, too. Well, I'm not going to do that anymore."

Tripp was still awestruck about his revelation concerning his feelings for her, and was trying to understand what she was trying to tell him. "What do you want to do, Amber?"

"I'm thinking about going back to school. Maybe I'll become a nurse practitioner, or perhaps a doctor. And you can't stop me. One way or another I'm going to do my life's work, maybe right here in Ukiah." She glanced at him, and then quickly away. "Well?" she finally whispered. "Aren't you going to try to talk me out of it?"

"I'd be wasting my breath."

She looked surprised, but not as surprised as she looked when he said, "I guess there's only one solution."

Her eyebrows drew down in consternation.

And he continued. "It looks as if you're going to make my life miserable one way or another. You might as well marry me."

She did a double take. "What?"

"I said I love you."

"No you didn't. That's not what you said at all."

He felt the strangest urge to grin. "It's what I should have said weeks ago."

"Really? You do? Love me, I mean?"

"I love you. I think I have since the beginning. Not when we were kids. The more recent beginning. I love you, and don't think that doesn't scare the hell out of me. But letting you walk out of my life scares me even more. So what do you think? And in case you're considering saying no, you should know that I've learned a thing or two this summer, too."

"What have you learned, Tripp?"

"I've learned not to take no for an answer." He touched his forehead to hers. "You were a great teacher. Now, what do you say?"

Amber didn't readily reply. She'd received four marriage proposals. This one wasn't the most romantic or the most original. It wasn't even the most eloquent. But it was the most heartfelt, and by far the most sincere. "You really love me?"

He nodded. "I truly love you. If you ask me to prove it, I'll spend the rest of my life doing just that." Slowly, he went down on one knee. Taking her hand in his, he looked up at her. "A woman like you deserves this done right."

"A woman like me?"

"Don't interrupt."

"My, you're bossy."

Under his breath, he muttered something about a pot calling the kettle black. She was more interested in what was coming next.

"You're perfect for me, Amber, inventive when I'm too much by the book, boisterous when I'm too serious, mouthy, well, most of the time. The truth is, I love that about you. I love most everything about you. Will you marry me, and live with me, and work with me if that's what you want to do? And love me? And have a family with me?"

Tears filled her eyes and her throat, but she nodded.

"Is that a yes?"

She wanted to smile, but couldn't. "Yes. This is a yes. To everything. I love you, Tripp."

He closed his eyes, and she wondered if he'd ever heard those words before. Slowly, he rose to his feet, and finally, he lowered his face to hers. Their lips met for the first time in two weeks. It felt like the first time ever. His mouth opened, hers softened. Breaths mingled, tongues touched, hearts joined.

It was heaven.

They were so different, physically. His lips were drier than hers, his body lean where hers was lush, flat where hers was curved, hard where hers wasn't. But inside, they shared the same beliefs, desires and philosophies. Amber loved that about him, but she loved the physical differences, too. They were perfectly delightful differences. She doubted she would ever tire of exploring them.

Music played in the background, and since the tree they were hiding behind didn't offer much privacy, they reined in their desire and kept the passion below the surface, where it simmered, waiting.

Waiting.

He loved her. Amber had hoped and prayed it was so. Her prayers had been answered.

"When?" he asked when the kiss finally broke.

Her mind swam as she tried to make sense of the question. "Pardon me?"

Tripp pulled her close to his side, an arm going around her waist. In the process, he got an eyeful of cleavage. She looked up at him and caught him looking. He had to clear his throat in order to speak. "When would you like to marry me?"

Amber smiled smugly. Tripp Calhoun wasn't a patient man. Looking out at the sky, now bright with stars and moonlight, she fit herself more comfortably in the crook under his arm. "How about tonight?" she asked.

He faced her. "You mean elope?" He was already shaking his head when he said, "A woman like you deserves a proper wedding."

She thought about the fairy-tale wedding she'd dreamed of all her life. In it, she'd imagined herself wearing a flowing white, beaded gown with a ten-foot train and a veil over her face. In her dreams, Emily was there, and her mother and father were deeply in love.

Amber gazed up at Tripp. This was reality. Suddenly, what mattered most was that she and Tripp were deeply in love. Tears filled her eyes. "I want to marry you. Tonight. Let's go to Vegas."

A smile of wonder found its way to his face. He reached for her hand. "Far be it from me to keep the lady from what she wants."

Two and a half hours later, Tripp placed a steadying hand on Amber's elbow. "You all right, Mrs. Calhoun?"

Still slightly groggy from her airsickness medicine, Amber nodded and peered at her dime-store wedding ring. "I'm wonderful."

"I'll buy you a decent ring," Tripp said, his voice husky with emotion. "Something with amber, or pearls, or anything you want."

"I have everything I want."

Hand in hand, they started down the steps of the bright pink wedding chapel where they'd just exchanged their vows and professed to love and cherish each other until death. Maybe even longer. In Amber's free hand, she carried the marriage certificate. In Tripp's was a Polaroid snapshot of him in his expensive black suit and her in her hussy-red dress with the slit up to here and the bodice down to there.

"You're a beautiful bride," he said.

"Thank you," she answered. She felt beautiful, and it had nothing to do with her dress.

A wolf whistle rent the air. From a car with its top down, a man called, "That's some trophy you got yourself, buddy."

"This isn't a trophy!" Tripp called. "This is my wife!"

He looked deep into Amber's eyes. It was true. He had something far better than a trophy wife. He had a woman as strong and stubborn as he was, a woman who was his equal.

Together, they started down the wide sidewalk. Amber had never felt so happy. Perhaps some day the remaining unsettling issues, such as her relationship with her mother, and Emily's disappearance, would be resolved. She prayed they would, but until then, and for always, she had the man she loved at her side. And he had her.

After all, love was the greatest trophy of all.

Don't miss the next installment of
THE COLTONS,
PREGNANT IN PROSPERINO
by Carla Cassidy
coming in April 2002.

One

"Wait..." Lana said. Chance turned and faced her expectantly, surprised to see a faint blush of color on her cheeks. "Your father's will...it just says you have to be married to inherit. It doesn't say anything about you having to stay married, right?"

"Yeah, so all I need is a temporary wife. You know anyone who might want to apply for the job?" he asked sarcastically.

The pink of her cheeks deepened. "Me."

Surprise swept through him and he stared at her wordlessly for a long moment. "Don't be ridiculous," he finally scoffed and started to walk again.

She quickly fell in beside him, her long legs almost matching his stride. "Why is it ridiculous?" she asked. "This ranch should be yours, Chance. I'll do it, I'll be your temporary wife so you can inherit."

He stopped walking and turned to her once again, utterly bewildered by her offer. "And why would you do something like that? What do you get out of the bargain?"

Maybe she figured to marry him then when he sold the ranch she'd get half the profit, he thought. What other possible scheme could she have for suggesting such a crazy scheme?

She drew a deep breath and he was suddenly aware of the press of her shapely breasts against the silk material of her white blouse. "A baby."

"A baby?" he echoed back with shock. "My God, Lana, if that's what you want, fall in love and get married, have babies and live happily-ever-after."

She frowned. "Chance, I'm thirty-one years old. I'm not dating anyone and I have no plans to marry, but I want a child." She raised her chin as her dark gaze held his and in the depths of her dark eyes he saw her strength…the same strength he'd always found attractive in her years past.

"Lana…"

"Think about it, Chance," she continued, her low voice ringing with a surprising boldness. "It would be perfect. We get married. You get your ranch and I get pregnant. Once we both have what we want, we divorce. No strings attached, no messy emotions."

Chance shook his head, trying to reconcile the woman before him with the shy, sweet young girl who'd been his confidante in one of the most difficult years of his life.

"Lana, I appreciate the offer, but I think working for my father these last few months have made you plumb loco. I can't marry you." He didn't intend to marry anyone. Again anger tore at him…anger at his father, who was, even from the grave, attempting to pull strings to control his life.

"It's a crazy idea and this is the end of this discussion." Without waiting for her reply, he stalked toward the house and the awaiting guests.